IS LANCER PUCKETT REALLY DEAD?

Share the experience of this young teen

as he finds out what lies beyond his untimely death.

By Eva Roberts

ISBN: 978-1-64314-365-1 (Paperback)
        978-1-64314-346-0 (Ebook)

AuthorsPress
California, USA
www.authorspress.com

Contents

Chapter 1

My New Hydro Hover Machine

This was a great day. The date was July 4, 2035, and not only was it a day to celebrate the independence of our great country, but it was also my sixteenth birthday! As I sat alone, perched on a large bolder about halfway between my house and the edge of town, waiting for my best friend, Jake, to arrive. I watched the fireworks display that was going on down at the town square.

The cool night air was a welcome treat, since earlier that day the temperature had skyrocketed to nearly a hundred degrees, and the humidity was so high that had it been any higher it would have been raining. But now, the night had brought with it a slight breeze that cooled my skin as it wafted over my sweaty body.

Our house was situated on a hill about a half mile from town, which gave me a great vantage point from which to view the colorful show.

People were scattered from the town to the edge of our five-acre property. They were all sitting on blankets and lawn chairs they'd brought with them to view the kaleidoscope of colors exploding in the starless night sky, which caused a strobe effect against the otherwise total blackness of this summer night.

This night in particular, it seemed to be blacker than usual for this time of night, but that was all right, because it was a great backdrop for the multitude of colors bursting high above with loud popping and crackling noises. The twinkling colors arched high above me and eventually fizzled out during their descent.

This was also my birthday, so I had an extra reason to be on cloud nine. You see, in our part of the country when students are almost sixteen, and if they've taken and passed the required flight instructions in the first semester of their senior year in high school, then their names are put into a government licensing computer, and they're automatically considered to be fully licensed on the day of your sixteenth birthday.

I was so excited because this meant I could legally fly my Hydro Hover Machine today, and I was anxious for Jake to get here so we could do just that. It seemed like I'd been waiting my whole life to get my license and my very own Hydro Hover Machine, and it just so happened that on that morning, my parents had presented me with my very own vehicle. But this being a holiday and all, my parents wouldn't let me fly it, because they said there was just too much to do in town to make sure the Fourth of July was respectfully honored. And they both wanted to be there when I had my first test flight. Dad told me there would be plenty of time later, but I'd been waiting all day, and I still hadn't had time to try out my new ride. To me, that was just too long.

Now if you don't know much about Hydro Hover Machines, they're vehicles powered by the same hydrogen energy made from the light nuclei and hydrogen atoms that were used in the atomic bomb that was detonated way back in the year 2006.

Even though this source of energy was ancient science, it was still considered one of the best sources of fuel to power most hover machines. The reason it was considered the best power source was because one could go from zero to two hundred and fifty miles an hour in twenty seconds, if somebody were crazy enough to accelerate that fast from a dead stop.

There were a few people in our town that still used the old-fashioned types of vehicles that drove with four wheels and ran on gasoline, but they were way outdated, and so were the people who drove them. I just figured they were too old to learn how to operate a hover machine and just didn't like change even though we've had hover machines for at least twenty years.

Mr. and Mrs. Jeb and Corrine Puckett are my parents, and they are well liked in our community, but like most common laborers, they struggle day in and day out to make a good life for us. Even so, they managed to scrape up enough money to buy me my very own Hydro Hover Machine. It didn't matter to me that it was already five years old, because it was new to me, and I knew all of my friends would be envious because it was newer than any of their hover machines, and it looked like it came right off the showroom floor.

My new ride had a fine metallic-silver paint job on the body, and the wings were painted a black onyx with red and yellow flame decals embedded along their edges, making it look like the wings were on fire. And since this was my first hover machine, I was just itching to get behind the controls and soar up into the clouds.

My lean, six foot, muscular body was quite mature for my age, and my dusty-blond hair hung shoulder length and blew lightly in the mild night air as I watched the magnificent fireworks, which were already well into their celebratory display, honoring the independence of our country.

I closed my eyes tight for a minute and tried to visualize myself high in the clouds. I couldn't wait for Jake to come so we could sneak off and take a night cruise in my new ride. No longer would I be confined to area within which my two feet could carry me. With my new hover machine, I could fly anywhere I wanted, and I couldn't wait to breeze over our town and all the neighborhoods in our community, just to see all of my friends looking up at me in awe, wondering if it was really me behind the controls of this marvelous machine.

Now, finally, at the grand age of sixteen, I thought of myself as macho, mature, and the man! And now that I had my own ride, I thought I was invincible, as most kids my age probably do. In my mind, no one was smarter, no one was more popular, and certainty no one was better looking than me. I thought I knew everything I would ever need to know. However, unbeknown to me at the time, I would soon learn, to my total amazement and sometimes absolute fear, that I knew practically nothing at all.

Chapter 2

Life Couldn't Be Better

My whole life was about to explode into such strange and unbelievable worlds that if people had tried to describe it to me that night, I'm sure I would have told them that they had more than just a few marbles loose, and that they belonged in a rubber room in some mental institution.

I couldn't see beyond my own little world, which revolved around my parents, my friends, school, and now my new fantastic hover machine. And the thought of getting behind my hover controls with my best friend, Jake, sitting next to me was the only thing on my mind at that moment.

I imagined us trolling around low over our quaint little town of Overton Mills, scoping out all the cute chicks, who I knew would think we were the coolest guys in town. Yet before we could do that, I wanted to get a little experience behind the controls of this magnificent piece of equipment so I wouldn't look stupid by doing something lame and end up stalling out or, worse, crashing in front of all of our friends.

I saw Jake wondering through the crowd of people sitting on large blankets scattered across the hillside watching the fireworks. He was looking all over for me.

"Lance? Lance, is that you over there?" he said, peering through the darkness in my direction. He called me Lance instead of Lancer because he thought adding the *r* at the end of my name made it sound too long.

I thought it was kind of funny that he felt the need to take off one letter, but if he thought it sounded better, then so be it, because I couldn't ask for a better friend.

He tried to speak softly, as he didn't want to draw attention to himself or to me. It was our plan to sneak out under the cover of darkness so we could try out my birthday present. I think Jake was as excited as I

4

was to ride in my new hover machine. I guess he thought if he was my wingman, then he had a better chance of impressing the girls, and maybe he was right. In any case, I didn't care if he wanted to impress the girls, because as far as I was concerned, he was my right hand wingman. We were as close as any two friends could be.

I was sitting just over a small ridge on top of my favorite bolder, which was just about fifty yards from the edge of town. I was looking into the black abyss above me as the townspeople below were setting up for the next round of bottle rockets and helicopters, which would soon light up the night sky. I didn't know what was taking Jake so long because he knew this was my favorite place to be and I had thought we agreed on this place this morning when he came over to see my new ride.

Lance was still picking his way through the crowd coming toward me. Again I let my gaze go upward, and still there were no stars in the sky that I could see, which I though was great because the dark backdrop made a perfect contrast for the colorful fireworks. But while waiting for the show to start up again there was kind of an ominous feeling that came over me. I thought for a second, "That's strange. Why should I be feeling this way?" Then I shook it off, thinking it was nothing, and I strained to see into the dark, watching Jake's progress toward me.

"Lance?" he called out hoarsely. "Lance, is that you?"

"Yeah, over here, but keep it down. What took you so long, buddy?"

He finally reached the perch of the big bolder I was sitting on.

"I had a hard time seeing in the dark, and the landscape looked so different with people sprawled out everywhere. But I'm here now so let's get going before more people come up here trying to get a better view." He playfully slugged me on my left arm, nudging me to go.

I didn't need any persuading. I couldn't wait to get out of there and up into the sky with the exploding fireworks. So I slid down the back of the bolder with Jake right behind me.

I was hoping Mom and Dad had gone to bed early, because I knew they both had to get up at the crack of dawn to work the next day in Old Man Vickers's factory. But just in case they were still up and sitting close by, I was praying that they didn't hear Jake calling me and decide to come over to where we were. He hadn't been so quiet, and he may have given us away, so that was all the more reason to get out of there quickly.

Now, anyone who was familiar with our quaint little town knew of Vickers's factory because that's where most people around here worked. It was a large storehouse and factory that took in old computers, stereos, all sorts of electronics and hardware, or just miscellaneous junk to recycle into new things, like stoves, dishwashers, radios, toys, and various electronics. It was hard work for Mom and Dad, as they worked on an assembly line, which was very tedious work for people their age, and you could see the fatigue in their faces when they got home each night. They worked from daybreak till long after the sun set, five days a week and most weekends. But never having had a real job myself, I didn't appreciate all that my parents had to sacrifice so that I could have a good life. My know-it-all self very seldom gave much thought for the struggles that a lot of people around here had to go through just to make ends meet. Although my parents did try to teach me to be self-sufficient and were always on me to get a job, I just kept putting it off, and I assured them I would get one just as soon as summer was over. But right now my only thought was of their whereabouts. If they hadn't gone to bed and were somewhere close watching the fireworks, like me, I hoped they hadn't heard Jake, I didn't want them to spoil our plans.

As Jake and I slid down the backside of the bolder, he commented on how he wished his birthday would hurry up and get here. Jake was slightly younger than me; he wouldn't turn sixteen for another three months, so he wasn't licensed to fly yet. But as my co-pilot, he could pretend that he was already licensed if he wanted to. Why I might even let him take the controls for a minute or two if I get tired, but I doubted that would happen.

Jake had dark brown curly hair and a shorter but stockier body than mine. We had the same dark brown eyes, and we liked the same things: hover machines, girls, and getting into mischief. I guess that's why Jake was my best friend. After all, we thought just alike almost all of the time.

His parents, Merle and Nancy Merlot, were very well off, and they were always ready to give a helping hand to those in need. And the good Lord knows that they have helped us out a time or two. Why, it was just last year that Dad had an accident in the factory and broke his right arm. He couldn't work for a full six weeks, and Jake's dad bought a whole month's groceries for our family to hold us over until Dad could go back to work.

As Jake and I headed for my house, I whispered to him, "Are you ready for this?"

"Yeah, old man," Jake said in a voice that was a little too loud for my liking.

"Good," I said with a finger up to my lips, indicating that he needed to keep his voice down. "Let's get out of here while everyone's eyes are stilled glued to the sky."

Hunched down and being as quiet as we could, we scrambled around the ridge and into Mom's organic vegetable garden, where the cornstalks loomed thirteen feet tall, which was the average height for corn in these parts, due to the highly enriched soil. There were also large melons, sweet potatoes, green beans, and squash just to name a few of the varieties of vegetables that grew right up to a fence that separated the garden from a swampy bog filled with cattails and water lilies.

After we crawled through a small hole in the fence, we carefully maneuvered around the bog, taking care not to slip into the swampy mud at the water's edge. This was quite tricky because we could barely see in the dark, except when a burst of fireworks gave us a little light for a few seconds at a time. Finally, after we managed to get past the bog without falling in, it was another seventy-five yards up a small, tree-covered hill to the back of my house.

The lights were all out, indicating that Mom and Dad had come home and had gone to bed, because if they had been out watching the fireworks, there would have been at least one light left on so they wouldn't have to walk into a dark house.

So as quietly as we could, we crept to the side of my house, where our big old dilapidated hover port stood.

For years, the half standing structure remained empty because our family couldn't afford any kind of vehicle, and Mom and Dad walked to and from work each day, regardless of the weather. Dad kept saying he needed to fix the supports on it before it fell completely down, and until he had a chance to do that, he didn't want to buy any kind of vehicle that might get crushed if the structure fell. But so far, he hadn't found the time or money to fix it. I don't think Dad wanted me to know that they couldn't afford a vehicle, so he just used that old hover port as an excuse not to get one. But now he'd have to fix it so I could have a safe place to store my new machine. Dad assured me that my hover machine would be safe for now, and he would get to it just as soon as he had the time.

So there, under the leaning roof of our hover port, sat my shiny new silver and black hover machine, just waiting for me to take it for a spin. I reached down into my left pocket and felt the cool metal key of my automatic door lifter and ignition starter. As I slowly removed my hand from my pocket, I anxiously fingered my key, making sure I knew which button was for the doors and which button was for the ignition. I excitedly pushed the triangular button in the center of the remote key, and the doors on both sides of the vehicle lifted simultaneously.

"Jake, get in," I said with a hushed voice. Jake slid into the passenger side, and I slipped into the operator's side. Again I pushed the triangular button, and both doors quietly lowered until I heard a soft click, telling me that both doors were securely closed.

"Don't you just love it?" I said. "This machine is just like the brand new models. I like the way the doors hardly make a sound when they close. Wasn't that cool? I was feeling so proud to show off my new machine to my best friend, Jake, that I could hardly contain myself.

"Won't the hydro lift wake up your parents when you start her up?" Jake asked as he fastened his seatbelt.

"No," I said. "We'll just use the fan and float mechanism and she will float to the street, and then we can start her up." I figured that with the fireworks crackling and popping all over the place, even if Mom or Dad did wake up, they'd probably think the sound of the atomic engine was just a loud firecracker.

"Now, it's important to know when operating a hover machine, that the higher you ascend, the faster your machine will fly, and if you want to fly slower, you must fly at a lower altitude."

"I know that, Lance," Jake said, a little irritated, because he had also taken the flying course.

I realized I probably sounded like a know-it-all. "Sorry, man, I didn't really mean anything by that," I said.

When we got out to the road, I fired up the atomic engine and hit the lift-forward button, and Jake and I gradually increased our speed, thus climbing higher and higher until we were high in the sky. Now we were breezing through the black clouds while sparkling flashes of green, blue, red, and yellow could be seen from the fireworks being shot off below.

We pretended that we were pilots in a war, and all these fireworks were enemy hover planes firing on us. We flew in and out of the flashing lights, laughing as we dodged them, avoiding being hit by the phantom enemy. Jake and I were having so much fun that we kept saying over and over again, "Life couldn't possibly get any better than this."

The night drifted by, and it wasn't long before the colorful explosions in the sky were gone, and we could see the first glimpse of the sun rising in the east. We knew we had to get back before anyone missed us, so grudgingly, I turned my new Hydro Hover Machine around and headed for home.

"Just drop me off in my backyard," Jake said. "I'll catch up with you later."

"Okay, I'll come around to pick you up about noon so we can cruise town," I said with a mischievous grin.

I wanted everyone to see my new ride. "And who knew? Maybe Jasmine would be in town too. At least I hoped so. Jasmine was a cheerleader with a great body and gorgeous long brown hair. Her eyes were a breathtaking shade of green that captivated me every time I saw them. I guess if I had to describe her eyes, I would say they were a brilliant emerald green. And they had a shine that would hypnotize even the least suspecting guy when he caught sight of their magnificent sparkle. Many a young man had been caught staring into those beautiful pools, then hastily turned away when they realized they had been caught.

I'd been trying to get Jasmine to notice me for almost a year now, with no luck. I guess that wasn't entirely true. She had said hi to me a couple of times in the hall at school, but she'd never really stopped to talk. It was my hope that she would finally take more notice of me and maybe even want to go out with me since I now had my own slicked-up, metallic-silver ride with fire streaked wings.

I slowed my hover machine down until I came to a halt over Jake's backyard. I lifted the passenger door by pushing an oval button on my dashboard, and Jake stepped out.

As he reached his porch, Jake once again said, "Man, oh man, life just couldn't get any better! What a day!"

As I lowered his door, I echoed out loud what he had just said. "You sure got that right. Life couldn't get any better than this. What a day!

Chapter 3

The Terrible Accident

I pressed the lift-forward button and slowly increased my speed to a slightly higher altitude as I left Jake's backyard. It felt really good to be flying alone in my very own Hydro Hover Machine, so I decided to take one more exciting fling around our neighborhood before I called it a night, even though it wasn't technically night anymore.

I accelerated to get to a good cruising altitude before I leveled off so I could take in the view. I was truly amazed at the sight of our tiny little town all sprawled out below, with many farms and small neighborhoods dotting its outskirts. The sun was just peeking up on the eastern horizon, and a slight fog reflected its rays over the landscape, showing me just how beautiful our town really was.

While cruising along at about five hundred feet above the ground and enjoying my ride and minding my own business, a fast moving shiny black hover machine appeared out of nowhere. It had duel engines, one on each wing, which lit up the sky, with bright red fire bursting from the back of each engine and leaving a trail of thick black smoke in their wake. The hover machine was beautiful and slick. It looked like some kind of speed racer that the wealthy around here like to go see on the weekends, but the operator of this machine was swerving erratically back and forth, as if he had been celebrating a bit too much the night before.

As I continued to watch this guy swerving back and forth, I didn't know what he was going to do next. I didn't know whether I should speed up or slow down or turn right or left to get out of his way. All I knew was that it looked like he was heading straight for me. It was almost as if he was trying to hit me.

The closer he got, the more erratic his flying became. I decided I better speed up, and I prayed that was the right decision. So I quickly pulled up hard on my steering handles and floored the atomic hydraulic peddles to rise as quickly as I could to get out of his way, but unfortunately the other guy did the same thing. I steered left, and then the other guy also turned toward my left. I thought, "Oh, my God. I think this guy is trying to kill me." I quickly made a very sharp right turn and kept turning until I had made a complete circle. I realized too late that the speed racer had mirrored my move, only in the opposite direction and we collided head on.

I felt the incredible impact of our two hover machines accompanied by a thundering explosion and a blinding flash of light. My vehicle went spinning and tumbling with tornadic speed down, down, down to the earth. Then everything went black.

I don't know how long I was out, but the next thing I knew I was being pulled through a long dark tunnel, and the farther in I was pulled, the brighter it got. I started seeing a multitude of colors, more brilliant than anything I could ever have imagined. The colors seemed to be encircling me, rotating around me in alternating directions, and warming my body. I could feel tremendous energy surging through me, but it was a good feeling, a joyous feeling. It made me feel invincible and alive, more alive than I've ever felt before. This tunnel was long and seemed to go on forever, but strangely enough, for some reason I didn't seem to mind. I was basking in this joyous warm feeling. My body was being electrified with a million tiny sparks of light particles, which seemed to boost my energy, and everything seemed so much more vibrant than I'd ever known or seen before.

My mind could not hold all the information and pictures that it was being shown, and I suddenly became very dizzy and disoriented. My thoughts were racing in all directions, and I became very frightened. My mind screamed, "Oh, God, please make it stop!"

Then, without warning, I was engulfed in a total blackness, and there was no sound or anything that my scenes could detect. I guess that was when I lost all consciousness.

Chapter 4

Back through Time

After some time, I awoke and tried to comprehend what had happened to me. I rubbed my eyes and inhaled deeply to clear my mind and try to maintain some sort of composure. When I looked around, I saw that I was in a very large, completely white chamber of some sort, with no windows and no doors. I went from complete blackness to now this totally white gigantic room, and as I continued to look around, I saw what appeared to be an opening to a corridor on the far side of the room. The corridor seemed to go on forever. However, it was kind of hard to tell, since everything was so white.

The floor was very shiny, almost mirror-like, but hard and cool as I sat there in a daze. I was still uncertain of where I was or if any of this was real. Then I decided this must all be a dream. "That's it. I'm dreaming," I said to myself. "This is just a dream, and sooner or later, I'll wake up."

Then, all of a sudden, strange images and thoughts came rushing into my mind, none of which I could comprehend, and my head felt like it was going to explode. I rubbed my temples, trying to make my thoughts stop whirling, since they were coming and going a million miles a minute now. I squeezed my eyes tightly shut and took in a deep breath, hoping that would quiet this jumble of thoughts that were threatening to blow my head wide open. Then the barrage of mindless thoughts seemed to quiet, and memories started coming back to me. I remembered the joy I had flying my very own hover machine with my best friend, Jake. Then, as the memories progressed, I remembered seeing that erratic hover machine operator heading straight for me. I then remembered a large explosion and a flash of bright light. It was then that the horrible realization came to me that I must have been hit by that other operator, who was flying like there was no tomorrow. I suddenly remembered that I hadn't had time to eject from my vehicle, and I remembered spinning and falling, then crashing to the earth.

"Oh no. Am I dead? No, no, no!" I screamed. "I can't be dead. This is all a terrible nightmare. Where am I?" Crazy thoughts kept running through my mind. "Where are Mom and Dad? Do they know I'm not home? Are they still asleep? Surely they must be missing me by now. I'm only sixteen. I can't be dead!" These dreadful thoughts kept pounding in my head that I was dead. "But, no, I can't be dead, or I wouldn't be thinking at all. I must be laying somewhere hurt and can't get back home. How come no one has found me yet?"

I was frightened, and my head was spinning and spinning, whirling out of control. My mind seemed to be going backward, and past memories started coming to me faster now. I remembered my fifteenth birthday, then my fourteenth, birthday, then earlier and earlier. Then my life seemed to be racing backward at warp speed. No matter how hard I tried to stop it, I couldn't. It now seemed that I couldn't keep any frame of logic in my mind at all. I tried to slow the barrage of compounding pictures and memories as they crowed in on top of each other, but I soon came to realize that was impossible. There was nothing I could do to stop these endless streams of nonsensical thought waves from coming into my head.

The memories kept racing by, and I soon realized that my own life's memories had vanished and that now I was experiencing someone else's life. The images flashing before me kept going backward further and further, and the people I was seeing were getting younger and younger. Then I saw yet another person's life, and on and on it went. I saw an old man lying on his deathbed, and then he was a young man, then a child, then a baby. As this strange movie kept running through my mind, I started to have the inexpiable feeling that all these people I was seeing were in fact me.

"This is impossible," my mind screamed. Those people couldn't have been me. Then, at the speed of light, I went back even further, to a time that was beyond this world. I was no longer in a human body. I had become pure light energy, consisting of billions of tiny atomic nebulae firing their electric charges, which formed the shape of my body as I passed through space from one galaxy to another, from one solar system to another and another. The beauty I beheld was so tremendous,

13

so brilliant, so breathtaking that mere words couldn't explain it. I saw planets with many colorful rings of mystical gasses encircling them. And I saw countless planets with many suns. There were also brilliantly colorful fields of stardust wafting through space that the normal eye could not bear to look at for its brightness. I saw planets bursting into a million tiny meteors, and I saw new planets being formed as red-hot suns exploded and then cooled.

This was amazing. I couldn't believe what I was seeing and experiencing. Wonder filled the space where fear had once been. I couldn't get enough. I wanted to know more, and I wanted to see more. Then all of a sudden the light energy, which had been my body, began to fade. I seemed to be drifting aimlessly and every wonderful thing that I had been experiencing suddenly vanished like it had never been there at all. Exhaustion engulfed every part of my being, and I felt a cold blackness engulf my mind again. My eyes became as heavy as lead and I could feel my body going limp as it fell to the cold hard floor in exhaustion, and again I fell into a dreamless sleep.

Chapter 5

Receiving the Bad News

It was six o'clock on the morning of July 5th when Officers Leroy Dunn and Joe Alverez knocked on the door at 726 Florence Drive, Overton Mills, Indiana.

"Jeb, wake up, dear. There's someone at the door," Corrine said to her husband as she reached for her robe at the end of the bed.

"What? What did you say, Corrine?" Jeb said, still half asleep and yawning widely between words?

Then another loud knock was heard at the front door downstairs. Quickly, Jeb got up, almost falling out of bed when he heard that second loud knock. As he looked around for his slippers, which had slid half under the bed, Corrine already had on her housecoat and had turned on the light in the hall light that led to the top of the stairs.

Another knock came, loud and hard. "All right. Hold your horses," Jeb said as he descended the ten steps to the foyer next to the front door.

"Mr. Jeb Puckett," Officer Dunn said as Jeb answered the door.

"Yes, that's me. What's going on, officers?"

By this time, Corrine had also descended the stairs, and she wrapped one arm around her husband's arm but stood slightly behind him.

"I'm Officer Leroy Dunn, and this is Officer Joe Alverez, and I'm afraid we have some very bad news for you this morning." Both officers removed their hats in respect.

Jeb's expression went from irritated to worried. His eyes questioned the officer's, not really wanting to hear the answer, because he knew it must have something to do with Lancer. Corrine tightened her hold of Jeb's left arm to brace for whatever bad news these two men had brought them.

"There was an accident early this morning, about five thirty," said Officer Alverez, his gaze compassionate. "And we are very sorry to report that your son, Lancer Puckett, was killed, as well as another hover machine operator. As close as we can figure, their hover machines collided about three quarters of a mile from here and crash landed just off Ward Lane, in the Hillshire District."

"No, that can't be true," Corrine blurted out. "Lancer is up in his room asleep. I'm sure of it. "She ran back up the stairs to check in his room. She flung open his bedroom door to find that his bed hadn't been slept in, and then she let out the most heartrending scream anyone had ever heard. "No! No! No!" she cried. Then she fell to her knees with her face in her hands, sobbing bitterly.

Jeb heard her screams and ran up the stairs to see if she was all right. He knelt down on one knee with her for a couple of minutes, then helped her up and walked her back down the stairs to the waiting officers as she shook uncontrollably in disbelief.

"Sir, Madam, we will be happy to drive you to the morgue so you can identify your son," Officer Dunn said.

"Yes, yes, Officer," Jeb said, his voice cracking as he tried to choke back his tears. Let us get dressed, and we will be right with you, Officers."

After arriving at the morgue, Mr. and Mrs. Puckett were led to a holding room where all lifeless bodies are brought prior to being sent to autopsy or to embalming. There they were met by the mortician who had just finished cleaning the blood off Lancer's face and arms so he wouldn't be so frightening when his parents were asked to identify him.

"Hello Mr. and Mrs. Puckett, I'm Dr. Frank Coons, the mortician. And I must tell you that the sight of your son's body might be a bit shocking, so I need you to prepare yourselves before I lift the sheet. I need you to identify his body. But again, if it is your son, you might not recognize him at first. The crash was pretty severe."

Corrine nervously held a handkerchief to her mouth, and Jeb held her hand as they walked, trembling, to a table on wheels that the mortician had led them too. There on the table was a body draped with a white sheet that had bloodstains all over it from head to foot.

"I apologize for the bloodstained sheet, but I didn't have time to get a new one before you arrived," Dr. Coons said softly.

Slowly and carefully, Dr. Coons folded back the sheet to expose the face of Lancer to his parents. A gasp of horror mixed with anguish escaped from the lips of both Jeb and Corrine at the same time as they looked at their son's bruised and mangled face. Corrine then buried her face in Jeb's chest and cried loudly in grief and anguish.

"I know this is hard," said Officer Alverez, who had walked in behind them. "But we need you to identify the body." Jeb just nodded his head in the affirmative and led Corrine away from the awful site.

Chapter 6

Meeting Estrella: Spirit Guide Number 1

"Wake up, Lancer," said someone in a soft, almost musical voice, which resonated in my head as I lay on the cold tile floor.

I was motionless and confused, and my head was pounding as I tried to remember what had happened to me. My throat was dry, and I dreaded the thought of moving or even opening my eyes. There seemed to be an underlying fear in my subconscious mind that the things I thought I had experienced with the crash of my hover machine were not a dream at all—going back through time, then traveling through space, and eventually ending up in this extremely large, empty, white room, which to me seemed more like a very clean prison. My mind kept telling me that somehow I had been thrust into some alternate demission, with no way to get back.

I silently but forcefully told myself that this was all a dream. But that nagging feeling kept telling me it wasn't. I was hoping beyond all hope that once I opened my eyes, I would see that I was actually back at home and in my very own soft bed. And all this crazy stuff that had been franticly churning in my head had just been a very weird and frightening nightmare.

I told myself, as I still lay motionless, barely daring to take even a breath, that it was just due to the stress of all the activity the day before. After all, it had been a holiday, and we had so much to prepare for the Fourth of July celebration, and on top of that, it was my birthday, and I was so excited to get my very own Hydro Hover Machine and take to the sky. So I reasoned that had to be the cause of me having such a crazy, mixed-up dream. "That's all it was," I told myself. "That's all it was—a crazy dream." "So as my mind returned to my Hydro Hover Machine,

18

I remembered that I had promised Jake that I would pick him up at noon so we could go buzzing around town, and this gave me a renewed excitement and a reason to wake up and open my eyes. So with this new understanding, I eagerly stretched my arms and legs and gave a big yawn. I rubbed my eyes and forced them to open so I could start my new day.

Once my eyes stopped fluttering from the bright light and finally came into focus, I quickly closed them tight again. "No, it can't be," I thought. I reasoned that the image of the large white chamber was still etched deeply in my mind from that strange dream, and I must still have been having it! I couldn't be awake yet.

So with great courage, I yelled, "Wake up Lancer!" I hoped that by hearing my own words out loud, I would finally wake up. And after convincing myself with a hard pinch to my left arm that I was awake, I slowly opened my eyes once more, and to my utter horror, I was still in this strange white room.

This was absolutely not my own bedroom in my own house in Overton Mills, Indiana, I thought, "Where am I? What is this place?" My mind agonized to find an answer, any answer, that would make sense of what was happening to me.

I was frozen stiff with fear, and I couldn't bring myself to believe what I was seeing, so I squeezed my eyes closed shut again, not wanting to wake up if this was my new reality. Then I heard it again. There was that soft voice, musically calling my name. So I mustered up the courage to open my eyes once more. And when I looked up in the direction that I thought I heard the voice coming from, I saw what looked like an angel coming toward me from that endless corridor I had seen earlier.

"It's all right, Lancer," she said. "It's perfectly all right. You're all right, my child. In fact, everything is all right."

I sat up and brought my knees up tight against my chest and tightly closed my eyes again. I repeated over and over again in my mind that this is not real! I tried to make some rational sense out of what was happening to me, but my mind had begun to whirl in every direction, making me feel like I was going insane. I was frozen—unable to move from the fetal position I was in, except for an uncontrollable rocking back and forth, as if I was trying to comfort myself like a mother rocks her baby. My single greatest hope was that I would snap out of this weird and frightening ordeal, but I didn't know how to do it.

Slowly I calmed the rocking, and I consciously opened my eyes again and forced myself to look around. Again I saw nothing but this very large empty white chamber with an endless corridor at the other end of the room. As I continued to scan the room, I didn't see the angel anymore, and I wondered if all this was some warped vision caused by my imagination.

All of a sudden, the most beautiful woman I had ever laid eyes on just seemed to appear from out of nowhere, right in front of me. She was petite, with long reddish-blond hair that flowed down to her tiny waist. Her skin was fair and very smooth, like a newborn baby's. She was dressed in a long white gown, which sparkled as she flowed gracefully around me, as if she were dancing to a beautiful ballet. As she circled around me, not once or twice, but three times, she looked me up and down very carefully, as if she were trying to take in every part of me to make sure I was all right or good enough. But good enough for what? Why was she checking me out so closely?

She then stopped right in front of me and looked me straight in the face, and when I looked into her eyes, I was struck at how beautifully crystal blue they were. It was as if she was trying to capture my very soul by drawing me into their endless pools of crystal-blue water that went on forever. But instead of being frightened, I began to feel refreshed and renewed from just staring into those liquid translucent orbs, and a sense of calm gently fell over me.

This beautiful lady's smile was warm and sincere, and her presence assured me that I had nothing to be afraid of. She offered her hand to me, and for some reason I took it willingly, and she help me to my feet. Again, she floated gracefully around me until she was satisfied with her inspection.

"Where am I?" I shyly asked her.

"Where would you like to be?" she said.

Still confused, and more than a bit amazed by all that was happening to me, I had trouble forming my thoughts into words. However, this beautiful angel that had just given me a thorough inspection must have sensed my confusion, because before I had a chance to say anything else, she said, "Let me be of assistance to you, young Lancer."

She then waved her hands above her head in a sweeping motion as she spun around in a circle, and suddenly the white chamber we had been in a second ago had vanished, and we were now in a beautiful valley nestled beneath a towering mountain with a roaring waterfall, which tumbled into a crystal-blue-green lake filled with water lilies and cattails. Trees of every color, shape, and size dotted the landscape, and flowers that I could never have imagined waved their lovely petals in the gentle breeze, their delightful fragrance wafting all around us.

Dumbfounded by this miraculous change of scenery, I managed to ask, "What is this place? I mean…where are we?"

She just smiled and said that this was one of her favorite places to be. She called it her heaven. And then she started dancing around and around in this beautiful field of flowers and singing some magical tune that was completely foreign to me.

"Wait a minute," I called out to her as she floated by me in a very playful way. "Who are you? I mean…what are you called? Do you have a name? What am I to call you? And how is it that you know who I am?" At that moment I had just remembered that she had said my name when she called me to wake up.

"Yes, dear Lancer, I am called Estrella, and I am your first spirit guide," she said in an almost whimsical, musical voice, so soft and so sweet.

"Spirit guide?" I called back as she continued to dance around the lake and waterfall. "Is that like an angel? Am I dead? I thought I heard you say that I wasn't dead. You know when you first came to me, didn't you say I wasn't dead? You said I was all right, didn't you?"

If I wasn't dead, what did I need a spirit guide for? Now the questions seemed to come tumbling out of my mouth with no coherent thought behind them at all and no way to stop them. I could hear myself speaking, but nothing seemed to make sense. My mind again had started whirling out of control, and I must have been acting crazy. I started pacing back and forth and around in circles, as butterflies fluttered around my feet and waist. I was wringing my hands and muttering incompressible words, trying to make sense out of all this, but I feared I would be forever lost in this hell of confusion and delusion, regardless of how beautiful it was.

Seconds later, I found myself sprawled out on a bed of pillowy flowers, where I had evidently flung myself in my desperate despair.

The next thing I knew, Estrella was standing next to me again. "You mustn't worry yourself so, young Lancer." Then, with a reassuring smile on her beautiful lips, she asked me if I was hungry? "I'm sure you must be famished after your long journey. Come and replenish yourself, for you will need all the energy you can muster for the fantastic journey you are about to embark on."

"Journey? What journey? Where am I going? Where are you taking me?" I said, not knowing how much more of this strange new world I could take.

"Oh, young Lancer, this is a wonderful journey, a journey that you must take partly alone, but you needn't fear, for if you are truly in need, I won't be far," she said. And again she told me to sit and replenish myself.

I leaned up on my elbow in the plush grass and flowers and looked around. "Where am I to sit?" I thought. "And what am I to eat? I don't see a table or a chair, and where is the food?"

She must have read my mind again, because immediately, as if by magic, with another wave of her hand there appeared two beautifully carved wooden chairs next to a large round table that was elegantly draped with a lovely white lace tablecloth. The tablecloth had tiny purple and yellow flowers embroidered on the edge. And in the center of the table sat a beautiful vase of scarlet-red roses.

"Sit here, young Lancer," she said, as she motioned to me to sit in one of the ornately carved wooden chairs.

I timidly followed her directions and slid comfortably into one of the chairs.

Again, she waved her hand, and out of thin air, two exquisitely hand-painted china plates and two crystal-jeweled, long-stemmed goblets and some beautifully etched silverware appeared on the table.

By this time, I was beginning to feel pretty famished, but where was the food? No sooner than that thought crossed my mind than the table was covered with an assortment of delicious foods. And everything I saw was one of my favorites dishes. I couldn't believe it! There was turkey and dressing, roast beef and mashed potatoes, cheese burgers, fries, pineapple upside-down cake, spaghetti and meatballs, pumpkin pie, and ice cream. How could she possibly know that all these foods were my favorites?

I quickly filled my plate and decided not to waste any more time trying to figure that one out, and I began eating. You can imagine my surprise when everything I tried tasted just like the food that my mom had always cooked. It was so delicious that even with this big spread, I didn't think I could get enough.

"Lancer," Estrella said in her soft, gentle voice. "There is much you must learn, and there are wonders to behold. This is a wonderful day for you, and I am so thoroughly overjoyed and delighted for you."

Again, her words came out in an all most musical tune, and I must admit that I was a little curious about their meaning. But since she hadn't offered an explanation to her strange words, my attention quickly went back to all the wonderful food in front of me. My mind, senses, and stomach were much more interested in all these delectable delights than in spending my curiosity on something that hadn't happened yet.

As I ate and ate, I couldn't believe how wonderful everything was. The turkey and dressing was delectable, and the deserts were so mouthwatering that I couldn't seem to get enough.

As Estrella sat across the table from me, it dawned on me that she wasn't eating anything, and I wondered why. Maybe she just didn't like my kind of food, or maybe she wasn't hungry. Then, to my utter surprise, she responded to my question, even though I knew I hadn't spoken it out loud.

She said to me in a lighthearted tone, which was again in the form of a musical melody, "Eating is a wonderful pastime, my dear Lancer, but I am so pleased that it isn't necessary for me. Oh, you needn't think that I never eat. It's just a rarity for me. I only do it at large gatherings or a special occasions."

Wow! This was all a bit crazy for me. I knew I hadn't spoken out loud, but she knew exactly what I was thinking. It must have been a lucky guess, that's all. A lucky guess. How could she have known what I was thinking? No one could read minds.

Then, for no apparent reason, she suddenly stood up from her chair and started dancing around the table while she sang and sang in her happy lighthearted style. "Dear Lancer, dear Lancer, there is much you must learn. Dear Lancer, dear Lancer, there is much you must see. Dear Lancer, dear Lancer, you must come with me."

Then Estrella suddenly touched me on my forehead, between and slightly above my eyebrows. And once she removed her hand, the beautiful landscape we were in, table, food, and all, slowly began to vanish. It was as if it were melting away from my mind and vision. I didn't know what was happening to me as I watched everything fade away. Even beautiful

Estrella seemed to be drawn farther and farther away, becoming tinier and tinier, until I could finally see her no more.

The next thing I was aware of was that I was utterly alone, standing in some kind of black void, and fear once again gripped me clear down to my very core. I called out for Estrella over and over again to no avail. "Estrella, where are you? Where are you?" I called, until I could no longer hear my own voice, as the coarseness chaffed my throat in this thick black void that seemed to engulf everything, even my own words.

Chapter 7

Into the Dark

I couldn't see anything in this oppressive black void I now found myself in. The air was extremely thick, like a dense fog on an early fall morning, but there was absolutely no light whatsoever. The lack of circulating air caused my body to sweat profusely. It was almost as if the moisture was being purposely sucked from my body. I wasn't sure if it was due to this oppressive atmosphere or because of this tremendous fear I felt at not knowing where I was or how to get out.

I held my arms out in front of me and felt nothing. Then I brought them straight out to each side, and both of my hands touched some kind of walls. Both walls felt rough but cool, and as my senses started to become heightened in this darkness, I could tell there was an earthy smell to their rough facade.

I cautiously ran my hands across the cool rough surface as I took a step forward. I discovered that there were strange, long, wiry things sticking out of the walls on each side of me. These things were damp to the touch, and some of them were actually kind of slimy, which made me instinctively pull my hands back and wipe them off on my pants to get the snot-like substance off of my fingers.

There were long ones and short one, curly ones and straight ones, fat ones and skinny. Some were very hard, but most were very pliable, and they were all tangled together. But the one thing they all had in common was that they reeked with a dreadful odor, like old musty wet newspapers that had been in a damp cellar for years.

"What is this wretched place?" I said to myself in a low whisper, as my worst childhood nightmares flashed before me.

I imagined all sorts of things, like prehistoric monsters from the beginning of time, hibernating in these dark chambers, or giant insects that could sense my tiniest movement and were ready to pounce on me for a little afternoon snack, or perhaps there were creepy crawly snakes here that were so poisonous that one bite could kill me in a matter of seconds. Or, I imagined, there were giant spiders ready to snag me up in their toxic webs and have me for dinner. These crazy thoughts were making me sick with fear, and I knew I had to find my way out of here as fast as I could. But which way should I go? Should I go straight ahead or back the other way? I didn't know which way to go, and I was shaking so uncontrollably with a fear that I thought I would be paralyzed and unable to move at all if I didn't decide soon.

Again I called out to Estrella in hopes she would come and take me out of this hellish place. "Estrella! Estrella, are you here? Estrella, where are you? Don't leave me here in this horrid place."

All of a sudden, a sense of calm came over me. This unexplainable calm just seemed to enter my body from the top of my head, and it traveled all the way down to my feet. There was still a little apprehension in my mind, but I was grateful that my fear had lessened, even though I couldn't understand why.

I had just enough calm that I felt I could breathe and collect my thoughts again. So I quickly decided I had better figure out how I was going to get out of this place before this darkness drove me insane.

This eerie black abyss had totally engulfed me, but there seemed to be an assurance from Estrella that she was right here with me, even though she never answered my calls and I couldn't see her. I felt like somehow she was giving me the courage I needed to move forward. So with both arms outstretched to my sides, and feeling the damp hard surfaces of the rough stringy walls, I again began to put one foot in front of the other.

As I walked forward, the tunnel became quite wide in certain areas and very narrow in other areas. In fact sometimes it became so narrow that I had to turn sideways just to squeeze through, but somehow I always managed to reach the other side where it became large enough to breathe again.

I also realized that my path had a continuous slight incline. And at that moment I heard the words in my head, "Follow the path up." I didn't know if I was being told this by some unknown being or if it was my intuition telling me which way to go. But instinctively, I felt that if I kept going up and didn't stray off this path into some other tunnel by accident, I would surely find my way out. So step-by-step, I slowly and cautiously moved forward and upward, feeling the cool damp walls on each side of me while I tried to ignore the feeling of the sticky, snotty substance that my fingers were being covered with.

After walking for what seemed like hours, I decided to take a short break, so I sat as close to the wall as possible, just in case there was something in this tunnel besides me. And I hoped if it came my way, it would crawl right past me and not even know I was here.

After what I thought to be about a thirty-minute rest, I carefully pulled myself back up to a standing position and breathed in as deeply as I could to fill my lungs with some much-needed air. I had to be nearing an exit from this horrible place, because the air seemed lighter and much easier to breathe, although there wasn't even the slightest hint of light.

So, with new determination, and depending solely on my instincts and faith to guide me, I started off again. But because I was so anxious to get out, I recklessly started jogging blindly down the tunnel, waving my arms this way and that, praying I would find my way out soon. Faster and faster my feet began to carry me, as I ran through this black hellhole.

Then, all of a sudden, with a smack, I ran square into a wall, and one of those hard sticks almost poked my right eye out. The pain I felt was excruciating, and I let out a yell that could have awakened the dead! In my hurry to get out of this terrible place, I had hit a wall right in front of me with such force that it knocked me back at least five and a half feet. When I landed, my arms instinctively went back to catch myself. I fell backward, and my hands and arms plunged deep into what appeared to be freshly plowed dirt, clear up to my elbows.

After recovering from having had the wind knocked out of me and nearly poking my eye out, I struggled to get my arms out of the dirt. I was able to get my right arm out by rolling toward my left side, but as I did this, the dirt started to give way, and my entire body felt like it was going to sink. At that point, I stopped moving and realized I had to think this thing through, because I feared I would be completely swallowed up by this endless sinkhole if I made the wrong move.

Frightened beyond words, I felt tears running down my grimy face, and I prayed with all my heart that I would be able to get out of this mess and reach daylight again.

Gradually, I mustered up enough courage to feel around with my free hand, and I was able to grab hold of one of those long, sticky vines protruding from the wall. After twisting it a couple of times around my wrist so I wouldn't lose my grip, I pulled with all my might, until I finally was able to drag myself onto firmer ground. Exhausted and scared, I lay face down on the cool, damp floor, which was amazingly comforting after almost being sucked into the center of the earth, or so I thought.

I was able to catch my breath and assess what injuries I might have suffered after crashing into the wall like that. And fortunately for me, the only real injury I could surmise was having my eye almost poked out when I made such a forceful impact with that wall.

My eye was throbbing now, and I could feel it beginning to swell. So I dug my fingers into the cool mud of the ground and managed to scoop out enough to make a mudpack. The mud was the texture of soft clay, so I was able to mold it into a round flat mud pie and place it on my eye. The coolness of my makeshift poultice seemed to help, so I held it there while I tried to shake off the loneliness and fear.

I wasn't sure how much time passed as I nursed my eye, but I knew I had been here much too long, so after a quick examination of my eye, and realizing that it was going to be all right, at least for now, I mustered up the courage to start again.

The wall I had run into was in front of me, so I crawled straight forward on my belly until I reached it. I stood up with my back against the wall and held my arms straight out to the sides again. Slowly, I took two cautious steps to my right, with my back still up against the wall, trying to feel if the path went on in this direction. I was happy to note that there was nothing but empty space, except for the wall I had my back against. Then I took two more steps, only this time I turned my body in the direction I was heading and stretched out both of my arms to the right and to the left of my body. I could feel the wall I had been leaning against with my left hand, and with two more steps I could also feel a wall on my right. And as I waved my hand in front of me, I realized that this was indeed another path and it appeared to be going up, not down.

"Ah-ha," I said to myself. This tunnel had come to a *T* in the road, or maybe it was an *L*, but at least it was still a path to somewhere and not a dead end.

The more I stumbled up this dark path, the more my eye and head began to throb. Walking had become very difficult, because I kept tripping over tangled vines and rocks, or at least I thought that was what they were. My eye was stinging as the blood vessels behind it pulsed with each heartbeat, and I couldn't tell if my eye was bleeding or if I was just feeling sweat running down my face. All this was just too much for me to take at that moment, so I backed up against the wall and slid down to the ground, exhausted.

I don't know how long I slept, but when I finally opened my eyes and realized I was still in this horrid tunnel, a sick and hopeless feeling came over me.

My body ached and my head pounded as I rubbed the place where that stick had almost rendered me sightless in one eye. I forced myself to stand up. At least I hoped I still had sight in that eye, but here in this awful darkness, there was no way to really be sure.

By now I had come to believe that I was underground and that those tangled vines were actually roots of some kind. But I had no idea how I got here or how to get out.

That once reassuring feeling I had that Estrella was leading me had vanished and had been replaced by a sick and confused feeling of uncertainty. But with or without Estrella, I knew I had to keep moving. So once again, I slowly drug myself forward, not knowing where or when this would all end.

Time seemed to creep by at a snail's pace, and after walking for some distance and following the curves of the wall that I had been clinging to, I could feel a distinct temperature change. This terrible dank place was definitely getting much hotter, and my clothes were now absolutely soaked with sweat. I also found the air to be much thinner here, which made it difficult for me to breathe, and if that wasn't bad enough, there was a very rank smell coming up from this filthy black corridor that threatened to make me retch.

I pinched my nose with the first finger and thumb of my left hand and tried to breathe through my mouth to keep from smelling that awful smell.

Suddenly, I realized to my dismay that the path I had been walking on had taken a downward turn. I choked back tears of anguish and fear as I held myself up against the now slimy, damp wall.

"Why is this wall so slimy?" I said to myself in a low, raspy voice. Horrible visions of giant black slugs entered my mind, and I sure didn't want to be slimed by one of those nasty creatures. So I clenched my fists and swallowed hard, trying to bring up my last ounce of courage. Then I prayed with all my might to whatever benevolent power there may be out there to help me out of this hellish place.

My knees were weak, and my legs were shaking, but again I heard the words in my mind: "Follow the path up, Lancer. Follow the path up."

I didn't know where this voice came from, but at this point I didn't care. It just made sense to travel up and not down. So I turned around and slowly headed back up the long treacherous tunnel, hoping I wouldn't make another wrong turn.

As I walked, I thought of home and the beautiful fireworks I'd watched on my birthday. I imagined my parents working in our garden, and I wondered if they even knew I was gone? "They must be so worried about me by now," I thought.

I also thought about my best friend, Jake. He would be so mad at me for not showing up at his house at noon like I said I would. Oh, man. I wished I was home at that moment.

After stumbling and crawling and inching my way through this black nightmare, I realized I was again coming into some lighter air. The air seemed to be getting fresher and was not so oppressive and hot. A renewed hope entered my soul as I took in a deep breath, filling my lungs to their capacity and then slowly exhaling.

It had seemed like an eternity since I'd found myself in this terrible place, but I now realized that this tunnel had become almost vertical, making it necessary for me to hang onto the tangled roots just to stay upright. I continued moving forward, pulling myself up and up farther and farther, until at last I began to see glimpses of light.

The roots in my path were now becoming more and more dense, making it almost impossible to pass. But after seeing the light, my strength became almost Herculean, and I was able to pull the roots apart and drag myself through.

A few minutes later, I began to hear a strange but somewhat familiar sound: plunk...plunk...plunk. And then it became deafening, like a thousand thundering horses running above me. For a split second, I didn't know what was happening. Then the torrents of water came rushing down over me, and it was all I could do to hang onto these slippery ropes coming out of the dirt walls.

I realized then that it was raining very heavily above me. There was a real fear I would be swept back down this awful hole and would drown, or worst yet buried alive by all the mud created by the downpour.

Again I tried calling for Estrella, which was no easy task, because my mouth and nose were being filled with a continuous flow of filthy water and mud. But somehow I managed to call out her name between gasps for air. "Estrella...help me...I'm drowning. I'm drowning!"

Then, to my total surprise, as if by magic, I could feel the warmth of the sun on my face and limbs. It filled my body and renewed my energy and strength. My senses told me I was lying on a soft bed of leaves or a freshly mowed lawn. And because of the sudden brightness after being in total blackness for so long, I could barely open my eyes without squinting to block some of the light out, so I decided to just keep them closed and enjoy the peace.

While I enjoyed this wonderful warmth on my face and body, there was an occasional slight breeze, which brought with it a hint of spring wildflowers.

My mind became relaxed and serene, and I thought, "If there is a heaven, this has to be it. If this is a dream, I sure don't want to wake up. Don't wake up, Lance. Don't let this dream ever end."

Chapter 8

Meeting Lord Aster: Spirit Guide Number 2

As I lay in the comfort of a sweet bed of leaves, I heard it again, that soft gentle voice calling my name. That strange musical melody, that could only come from my spirit guide, Estrella.

At first I was overjoyed to know she was there, but then I remembered with horror that it was Estrella who had put me into that horrid, smelly black tunnel in the first place.

I put my hands over my ears and tried to bury my head deeper into the pile of leaves that I was laying on.

"Lancer. My dear sweet Lancer. It's time to get up," she said in that enchanting musical voice.

"No, I don't want to get up. I don't want another nightmare to happen to me," I screamed.

"Lancer," she said. "Don't you trust me?"

"Why should I? First you tell me I'm all right and that I'm not dead, and then you feed me this wonderful meal. Then you take it all away and throw me into a very frightening black abyss that I thought I would never get out of. You told me that you were my spirit guide. I thought you were my friend. Where were you when I was all alone and needed your help? If I'm not dead, then I want to wake up right now in my own bed."

"My dear Lancer, I am your friend, and I was there with you the whole time you were experiencing what you called a hellish black void." Her voice was sweet and calm. "It was I who whispered to you and told you to follow the path up. It was I who gave you the strength to keep going when you thought you couldn't go a step farther. Lancer, that was an experience that you needed to go through in order to prepare you for your work ahead. My dear Lancer, open your eyes. I have someone very special here who is anxious to meet you."

I wasn't sure I wanted to meet anyone else. Maybe this other person would torture me even worse than Estrella did. But something in her soothing voice reassured me that it was all right, so I slowly opened my eyes and sat up.

At first, as I looked around I didn't see anyone, but what I did see was almost impossible to believe. Towering high above me was a humongous yellow flower with equally humongous jagged leaves. Next to the yellow flower was another long stem, and on its end was a huge, white, fluffy dandelion puff.

Then I realized I was sitting on a large dandelion leaf in the midst of an ocean of leaves, which had fallen from a skyscraper-size tree just a few yards away. I could only see part of the tree because my view was blocked by what appeared to be a jungle of tall grasses and weeds that loomed all around me like a menacing forest. It reminded me of the Amazon rain forest that I had read about in school, and I feared that I would be caught in this tangle of weeds, trees, grasses, and vines forever, with no one to lead me out. Was this another kind of hell, only with fresh air and sunlight?

I could hear the deafening sound of insects and small animals, like crickets and bullfrogs, reverberating in my ears. The relief of being out of that smelly black hole was soon lost in the fear of being eaten by some prehistoric insect or rodent.

A few minutes later, two figures of light appeared high in the sky and slowly descended to where I sat on my giant leaf. Then to my complete amazement these light figures seemed to materialize into solid forms as if they had been beamed in from some distant star.

As I watched in amazement, these two luminescent beings began to diminish in their brilliance. And once their luminosity solidified, I recognized Estrella standing next to a tall man, who was very plump and had a long, silvery-white beard. He had the kindest smile I'd ever seen with the exception of Estrella. This large, strange man was dressed in a full-length orange robe and held a long staff with a large sapphire gem on top. Even though he was an older man, there seemed to be a playful yet wise youthfulness about him. He raised and lowered his bushy eyebrows as he closely examined me, and then he nodded, as if giving his approval.

He then motioned for me to stand up, so I obediently did without question. And as the three of us stood on this gigantic leaf, I could feel the tremendous compassion that they both seemed to have for me.

"Lancer, I would like you to meet Lord Aster," Estrella said with a sweet smile on her lips. "He is going to take you on your next journey. He is very wise, and any questions you have, I'm sure he will be pleased to answer them for you. I must be going now. I have many things to do. Good-bye, sweet Lancer."

"Wait. Where are you going? Don't leave!"

I didn't want her to go. Even though this man seemed kind and good, I felt a special bond with Estrella, and a sense of security with her. All thoughts of her sending me to that black abyss had vanished, and I feared I would never see her again.

"You will be in good hands with Lord Aster," she said. "Have no fear, and learn well, my sweet Lancer." Then she faded away in a shimmery mist.

As I timidly faced Lord Aster, I shyly asked, "Can you please tell me, what is this place, and how do we get out of here, your magnificence, or your kingship, or what should I call you? (He looked like a king to me, with that jeweled staff and all).

"Lord Aster is just fine. You may call me Lord Aster," he said. But he did not speak. No words came from his mouth. He just made his words known in my mind.

"This is too weird," I thought. "How can he possibly speak to me without using real words? And how did I understand what he was saying, since he didn't speak using his mouth?"

"My son, this is indeed another world that you will learn about. There are many things that you cannot understand as of yet, but have no fear, you will be prepared before your first assignment," he said with authority. Again, he spoke to me, but his lips never moved. His statement was made known to me telepathically. I was dumbfounded and thought that he must be some kind of ventriloquist—or a God!

As I was standing there trying to figure out how he did that, I began hearing a loud buzzing noise coming straight for us. And when I looked up to see where it was coming from, I saw to my horror what appeared to be a prehistoric, gigantic bumblebee encircling the dandelion that loomed over us.

I crouched low with my hands over my head and screamed, "Make it go away. Make it go away!"

"It's safe in here, Lancer," said Lord Aster, again without uttering a word.

"In here? What do you mean, in here?" I screamed. "We are outside with that thing."

And again he silently said to me, "It cannot harm you while we are in here."

I slowly peeked through my crossed arms that were folded over my head and looked up to see what he was talking about, and to my surprise I saw that we were enclosed in some kind of translucent bubble. "Is this a force field?" I asked him.

"I suppose you could say that." And like before he spoke to me without using actual words.

I tried to see if he was moving his lips at all, but it didn't appear so, so I asked him, "Don't you ever use your mouth to speak?"

Telepathically, he said, "Why should I, when it isn't necessary to use my mouth. It's just a waste of time and energy."

"Do you ever eat?" I wondered silently.

"That also isn't necessary for me. Let's go, young Lancer. I want to show you this amazing world."

Realizing that there was indeed something very strange and very special about Lord Aster, I nodded my consent as I looked up to see that giant bumblebee sucking nectar from the flower at the top of this plant we were on.

Lord Aster stepped down from the leaf. Then he motioned for me to follow. As I proceeded to step from the leaf, I almost slipped from a pool of water that was left behind from the morning dew. I was amazed that we were so tiny, or maybe we were the right size and everything else here was so huge. But for now I kept my questions to myself, even though I knew that was useless because this great being was able to read my every thought.

Hours seemed to pass in relative calm as we trudged endlessly through this vast jungle, and my legs were getting extremely tired as we climbed over one big dirt mountain after another. We also had to cross over large crevasses and fight our way through an endless barrage of sharp sticky weeds and coarse grass stalks. At least I had to. Lord Aster, who was in front of me, seemed to have no problem at all. It was as if all this thick growth just parted for him to pass by but quickly sprang back in place, making it really difficult for me to follow.

"Isn't it time to rest, your Lordship. I mean, Lord Aster? Surely it's lunchtime by now. I'm starving. Did you happen to bring some food?"

He motioned for me to sit and to hold out my hands, and then he reached over to an unfamiliar plant and plucked a large fruit from its stem and handed it to me.

I had never seen this kind of fruit before and definitely never a fruit so big. It was ruby red and shaped kind of like a banana. I was a little hesitant to taste it because it was nothing I had ever seen before, but since I was really hungry and Lord Aster had given it to me, I decided what the heck and took a small bite. The juiciness of this fruit was like that of an orange and the taste was like a fresh pineapple mixed with strawberries. It was cool and refreshing and very satisfying. I gobbled it greedily, making sure I didn't miss any part of it. I even licked the juice from my fingers, savoring every sweet drop.

"Slow down, young Lancer," said Lord Aster in a soft but stern voice. "It is not necessary to eat so fast. This fruit will give you plenty of energy to last you a very long while."

"This is a wonderful fruit. What is it called?" I asked.

"It does not yet have a name. It just came into existence since you were hungry," he said, once again using only his thoughts.

"Wow, this is incredible. You mean to tell me that because I was tired and hungry, my thoughts created this just for me?"

"Yes, your thoughts are very powerful, so be very careful what you think."

As I sat there savoring the sweetness of this wonderful fruit and wiping the juice from my chin, a new energy began to awaken in my body, and I marveled at how this wonderful new food could enliven me so much. I felt like I could climb any mountain or run a thousand miles. I didn't feel hyper. I just felt strong and energized. It made me feel really good inside. And all of the pain I had when I was in that black hole had completely vanished. I could even see really well out of both eyes.

"If you like, young sir, you can give it a name. What shall you call this new fruit of yours?" Lord Aster said. As always, he telepathically made his words known to me, so by now I had come to expect that this was the way he preferred to communicate.

"Hmm. Let me see. I think I will call it the life fruit. You know—because it's the fruit that just came to life for me and also because it makes one feel like they have come back to life after being so tired and hungry." I was proud of the name I had given this new fruit, and I thought it was funny that I got to name it, so I laughed out loud with delight.

Lord Aster laughed with me, only this time it was a real laugh, a hearty laugh, and I watched the aged wisdom and youthful playfulness in his knowing eyes.

Then, startled back to the awareness of where we were, I felt the earth beneath us begin to shake. Were we having an earthquake? Then came the thunderous sound of many feet marching closer and closer to us, and my irrational mind visualized a furious throng of vicious armies coming to kill us.

"What's that?" I whispered with a shaky voice and wide eyes as I searched the landscape through the towering growth of weeds and grasses. I could feel fear rising up in my throat, and I wanted to jump behind the large weeds to get out of sight before that horrible throng reached us.

But instead of diving into the weeds I looked to Lord Aster for reassurance, and to my surprise, he just sat there with a peaceful look on his face. Didn't he hear that thunderous noise? Had he suddenly gone deaf? But even if he had, didn't he feel the earth shaking beneath us?

I tried not to appear frightened, because deep inside, I knew that I was safe as long as I was with him. But that thunderous sound and the vibration of the ground made me want to scream at him saying, "Lord Aster, don't you hear it, don't you feel it? What do we do?"

Then I remembered that bumblebee and the translucent bubble we were in that protected us from it. This gave me a sense of comfort, until I realized that we no longer had that force field around us. I wanted to scream, "Put it back up! Put it back up!" but I didn't. I just sat there paralyzed.

I glanced back again at Lord Aster. There was a gentle smile on his face, and his eyes were partly closed. I wasn't sure if he was asleep or in some kind of trance, but he seemed to have no fear.

I wanted to be like him and just ignore that awful sound thundering toward us. But I couldn't ignore it, and my body trembled uncontrollably.

I strained to look through the thick growth behind us to see what was coming, as the sound of many feet grew louder and louder. My heart was beating so hard and fast that I thought it was going to beat right out of my chest. My nerves were close to a breaking point, and still Lord Aster just sat there as if he were basking in the midafternoon sun without a care in the world.

Then all of a sudden an army of giant black ants came pushing its way over and through the thick grass. I held my breath as they marched in single file right next to us, carrying leaves and sticks on their backs. The feelers on their heads moved continuously back and forth as their sharp hooked jaws cut through the tough undergrowth so they could pass.

To my surprise and relief, they paid no attention to us. It was as if they were on a mission, and nothing and no one was going to distract them from accomplishing it.

After the last ant had gone by, Lord Aster stood up, then raised his arms high above his head in a stretching motion and said to me, "It's time to be on our way now. The ants have made a nice path for you to follow so you won't have to fight so hard to get through."

I wasn't sure that he had even noticed the ants, because he seemed to be in some kind of trance the whole time they were marching by us. And I wasn't thrilled about following them on their own path, but since I didn't really have a choice unless I wanted to find myself alone again—and I didn't want that—I decided I better do as he said. So I got up and followed Lord Aster as he walked calmly in the direction of the ants.

As we were walking along at a pleasant pace, I asked Lord Aster where our translucent force field had gone. He told me (in his silent way) that we didn't need it anymore. He then put his arm around my shoulder as we walked and assured me that if we found ourselves in extreme danger, he would bring it back again. This was a big relief to me as we followed the path made by the ants.

After climbing out of a large crevice and over a small hill, we could see the ants crossing a large river. The ones that had been carrying the sticks used them to make a bridge, while other ants floated across the water on the leaves.

"Wow! Would you look at that," I said. I marveled at how resourceful they were.

"Yes," said Lord Aster. "Ants are very resourceful, and they work together to accomplish goals that would otherwise be impossible. But now, young Lancer, it is time to rest because you have a long journey ahead, and soon our time together will come to an end. If you like, we can take this time to talk for a while. I'm sure you have lots of questions."

As we sat on the soft grass that the ants had conveniently trampled down for us, many questions started springing up in my mind. The fact that Lord Aster had just told me that our time together would soon come to an end just went in one ear and out the other without registering.

"Lord Aster," I said. Why is everything so huge here? I mean, how can weeds and grass be so large that we can sit on a single leaf and still have plenty of room to move around on it? And how come the insects are humongous? Are they so big, or are we that small?"

The clear glistening pools of his eyes showed boundless compassion and great wisdom as he listened to my questions. "Young Lancer, have you not noticed that this is but another dimension of the world you are from?"

My eyes grew big with surprise, and I wondered how this could possibly be. This world looked nothing at all like my world. We didn't have weeds and insects as large as people, so how could this be part of my world?

"You see, young Lancer, this is the world of the insects. This is how the insect views the world you live in."

"Okay, if this is so, then what about that black hole I was in before I met you? That didn't look anything like my world."

"Oh, but it is the world you come from, my dear son. You were in one of the vast trillions upon trillions of underground canals made by all the various life forms that live under the earth. The canal you were in, dear Lancer, just happened to be that of a Lumbricina, or a common earthworm. The amount of life living under the earth's surface is unfathomable to you right now, but you will soon become aware of many more forms of life and many more worlds in your world than you ever believed to be possible."

"Why…I mean, how can we be so small as to be the same size as the ants?" I asked."

"Young Lancer," he said. "Thoughts are very powerful things. Don't you remember me telling you that thoughts are very powerful? You see, my young lad, everything, before it was, was first a thought—a thought from pure consciousness."

"But I never thought of myself as being this small," I said.

"Oh, but I did, my son. I wanted you to experience and see what it is like from the insect's point of view. You see, the smaller you are, the faster your energy is moving. And the speed of your energy is what determines what form and size you are to become. If your mass is large, then your energy moves at a slower rate, but if your mass is small, that means that your energy is moving at a much faster rate." Lord Aster parted the tall grass with his jeweled staff. "Look over there. What do you see?"

I looked through the opening he had made for me, and I saw what looked like two very large hairy tree trunks. "What are they?" I asked. "They don't look like the normal tree that I'm used to seeing in my world."

"Young Lancer," Lord Aster said as he laughed out loud. Then he returned to communicating with his mind. "You didn't look all the way up."

So I looked up as far as my neck would let me without falling backward. And when I finally took in the entire view, I was surprised to see that it was a boy—a boy wearing blue running shorts and a white T-shirt. And this boy looked just like my best friend, Jake. "That looks like a large, lifelike statue of my best friend, Jake," I said.

"That is your best friend," Lord Aster said.

"What? How can that be? Why is he so big, and why is he not moving?"

"He is moving," Lord Aster said. "He is walking across his backyard. It's just that his mass is so large compared to ours that he appears to be standing motionless. That's the way everything in the universe works. The larger the mass the slower the energy vibrates. To Jake, he is walking at his normal rate of speed, but to us he looks motionless. Now, young Lancer, if your friend saw someone as large to him as he is to us, that person would appear to him to be stationary, and he could run laps around the person, just like we could run laps around Jake if we chose to. The speed of energy, which is actually trillions upon trillions of tiny light particles, is what brings everything into manifestation. Another word I like to call these light particles or energy is thought-trons. Do you understand now, my boy, that everything is created through thought-trons or energy or light particles. And that the speed by which these thought-trons vibrate is what brings everything into existence in a particular form?"

All this scientific talk was too much for me. "You mean to tell me that we are in Jake's backyard?" I asked with amazement.

"Yes, young Lancer. I just told you that."

My mind was again whirling with this new information. Then I remembered seeing the ants crossing that river, and I knew Jake didn't have a river in his backyard. So I blurted out, "But Jake doesn't have a river in his backyard, and we saw those ants crossing a river!"

"Lancer, didn't you hear anything I've told you," Lord Aster said with a touch of impatience in his tone, but then he quickly softened his voice and smiled as he continued. "Since we are so small, what appeared to be a river to us is, in reality, only a trickle of water in this yard." He then told me that Jack had been watering his garden and that river was just a little run off that hadn't been absorbed in the ground yet.

"Oh, okay. I think it's beginning to sink in," I said. "But I have one more question for you. How is it that you can speak to my mind without using real words, I mean without using your mouth to say words?"

"My child, as all life evolves, the spirit evolves with it, and when you get to a certain point in your development—or evolution, I should say—words are no longer necessary. Like I have said before, your thoughts are very powerful, but at this stage in your evolving, you have not yet figured out how to use your thoughts in this creative way."

"Okay," I said. "I believe that, but how do I develop my thoughts or my mind so that I can do what you do?"

"You must meditate, dear Lancer. You must learn to quiet your mind of all thoughts so that your awareness or intuitive insight can be awakened. It is through full awareness that all things were created. It is through full awareness that all things are possible."

Now with my interest piqued, and hopeful that someday I would be able to do what Lord Aster could do, I wanted to jump-start my evolution. I wanted to be able to read minds and talk without speaking just like him. "But how does one meditate?" I asked. "Can you teach me?"

"Not so fast, my son," he said. "I can give you the steps you need to meditate, but full awareness doesn't come overnight. You will find that, through meditation, you will gradually lose your selfish desires. Your thoughts will be transformed into what you can do for others and not what you can do or have for yourself."

I became disheartened a little because the reason I wanted to evolve was so I could read minds and talk without speaking words, but I guessed those were selfish things, and in learning to meditate, I would lose those desires. Anyway, I knew that learning to meditate was a good thing, so again, I asked Lord Aster to teach me.

"First you must sit erect and breathe deeply, cleansing yourself of all negativity," he said. "Then focus your concentration at the point between your eyebrows but slightly above them, then concentrate on one thing, such as love, peace, or compassion, or perhaps strength or good health, but make sure it isn't a negative or selfish thought. Your mind at first will want to wander to all sorts of things. It tries to distract you from your goal. Once you realize that it has wandered, gently and kindly bring your mind back to your original thought. Then, after a while, and I must say it could be a long while, you will become accustomed to concentrating and focusing on that one thought that brings you to your center. Your center is that special place within you, where all existence has its origin. It is that place where your intuition lives, and your intuition speaks only the truth to you. This is meditation, young Lancer, and once your intuition and awareness are fully developed, then you will be able to read minds, speak without actually using your mouth, and create anything you could possibly imagine. You will be a creator, my son." Lord Aster patted me on the head.

After listening intently to all that Lord Aster had been telling me and trying to take everything in, I found myself becoming very tired, and my eyes fought to stay open.

"Our time together is soon to be over, my young lad," Lord Aster said with a compassionate smile. "You must get some rest."

I nodded a yes as I watched him close his wise, peaceful eyes, and I wondered if he had gone off to some distant celestial place. And with my mind full of many wonderful new possibilities, I lay my head on the soft grass and was soon snoring my way to a wonderful bliss.

Chapter 9

The Underwater Cave

My dreams were alive with everything Lord Aster had told me. And in the comfort of what my mind thought was Jake's backyard, I recalled what Lord Aster had told me about energy, or what he called thought-trons. He said that thought-trons created absolutely everything. And through diligent meditation, someday I too would be able to do the things he could do.

Still a bit groggy, I stretched and yawned to wake myself up. When I opened my eyes and sat up, I still felt like I was half asleep, because my vision was a bit blurred, and it was no longer light outside. An icy chill ran through my body, and I figured that Lord Aster and I had slept too long, because the night air was cool and very damp, and I thought that was what was making me shiver so much.

As I looked around, still trying to focus, I saw little flashes of silvery-blue light whizzing by back and forth a short distance away. I wonder what that was. Maybe lightning bugs. Yes that had to be it. They were little lighting bugs, I reasoned, because they seemed to be one place one minute and then someplace else the next.

As my eyes finally adjusted to the diminished light, I could see to my astonishment that I wasn't in Jake's backyard anymore. But where was I? And where was Lord Aster?

"Lord Aster," I called out, with a blast of bubbles and a strange gurgling sound escaping from my mouth. This surprised me, and I wasn't sure if I was hallucinating or still dreaming, so I called out again. "Lord Aster, where are you?" And again I was astonished to see bubbles coming out of my mouth, accompanied by that strange gurgle that didn't sound at all like my voice.

Then I remembered Lord Aster saying something about our time together coming to an end, and again a sinking sick feeling came over me. "Not again!" I lamented. "I don't want to be alone now. I'm afraid. Where am I? What is this place?" My mind was being invaded by horrifying thoughts again—the same kind of thought that tried to consume me when I was in that worm canal.

"You have to get a hold of yourself, Lance," I thought. I then remembered Lord Aster teaching me how to meditate. He said, "Take some deep breaths and focus your thoughts on something good. This will quiet your mind, and once your mind is still, you can ask your questions, and the universe will give you the answers you are looking for."

As I tried to take in a deep breath, I felt a gush of cold water rush into my mouth and into my lungs. I started choking and coughing. I nearly drowned myself, except my choke reflex caused the coughing to send torrents of bubbles blasting from my mouth. This allowed something to kick in, and my breathing became less strained.

When the coughing finally stopped, I managed to gather some measure of composure so I could try to figure out what had just happened to me.

My body felt weak, soar, and uncomfortable from fighting to get the water out of my lungs. But why had water entered my mouth in the first place? I was just trying to take in a deep breath so I could meditate. It was not like I was underwater or anything, so it was incomprehensible to me why I had choked.

I shifted my body to find a more comfortable position so I could clear the cobwebs out of my mind, and I noticed a wave of ripples all around me, which seemed to emanate from by body. I also noticed that there was a feeling of buoyancy to my body, which made me feel almost weightless. Then, with a shock, I realized I was underwater. Underwater! "How can I be underwater and still talk and breathe?" I wondered in amazement. I then realized that if I just breathed normally through my nose, this water I found myself in was somehow blocked from entering my lungs. But still I didn't understand how I could breathe with no air. Perhaps I had something in my sinus cavity that resembled the gills of a fish. I wasn't sure, but at this point I was just happy that I was able to breathe at all.

Just then, those silvery-blue lights went right past me, and I could see that they were little, transparent florescent fish. As I looked around

I gasp, realizing that I was in a very large underwater cave, which made me start coughing torrents of bubbles again. When I finally stopped coughing and regained some sense of composure, I saw that somehow I had been deposited high upon a very narrow cliff, about fifty feet from the cave floor.

As I carefully looked over the edge, I could see beautiful beds of crystals in all sizes and shapes and colors on the ground below me. Somehow they were emitting a soft glow, which made it possible to see in this otherwise dark cave. As I carefully surveyed my new environment, I could see several dark holes in the cave walls, but I didn't know if they were tunnels that led out to the sea or just black holes, where some strange, never-before-seen, aquatic life-forms made their home.

I scooted myself as far back up against the wall as I could, so I was sure I wouldn't fall off, and I wondered how on earth I was going to get down. Not to mention how I was going to get out of here once I got down, if I ever did.

"Maybe this is where I'll meet my end," I thought. "No! Snap out of it, Lancer Puckett!"

Then, as I leaned my head against the cave wall, I tried to remember everything I had been taught so far by Estrella and Lord Aster, hoping it would give me a clue as to what I should do next.

I remembered Lord Aster telling me that there were many worlds within my own world, which I would soon learn about. And then I remembered that awful terrible dark worm tunnel I was in, and the land of the insects that wasn't quite so bad.

"This must be the land of fish," I reasoned. "And I must have been put here to see how they live, but that still doesn't tell me how I'm going to get out of here." I decided I would just sit there until Estrella or Lord Aster came to rescue me. I mean, what else could I do? They had to know I was here. After all, it had to be one of them who put me here. So I closed my eyes and tried to think of myself as being warm in this cold underwater cave.

Chapter 10

Thaumas The Dolphin

Shaken awake from the frigid water I was in, and remembering I was still sitting on that ledge, I thought I heard a muffled voice calling my name.

"Lancer? Lancer, my boy, are you in there?"

I wasn't sure if I was imagining it or not, so I leaned as far to the edge of the narrow cliff as I dared and cupped my right ear with my right hand as I held onto a protruding piece of stone that was securely attached to the perch that held my life.

Then I heard it again. "Lancer, my boy, are you in there?" It was a strange, deep, gargled voiced.

It didn't sound at all like Estrella or Lord Aster, but maybe it was because the voice was underwater.

"Lancer, if you're in there, please come out."

"Who are you?" I asked, with another blast of bubbles.

"I'm your next guide, sent to you by the one and only great supreme consciousness—the creator of the universe. I'm called Thaumas, my lad, and I've been looking all over for you!"

Wow! The one and only great supreme consciousness, the creator of all, sent this guide to me. Well, it was about time I was rescued. If the great supreme consciousness knew I was here, why didn't he send someone sooner? And why did my guide have to look all over for me? He should have known right where I was, if the creator of all that is sent him to me. Well, for the time being, I decided not to look a gift horse in the mouth and not to question him about why it took him so long to find me.

"I can't come out," I said. "I'm stuck on a ledge about fifty feet from the ground."

"Well, my boy, didn't you learn how to swim when you were a wee lad in Overton Mills?" he asked.

"Yes, and I'm not a wee lad. I'm sixteen," I said with a bit of sarcasm. I didn't much like being called a wee lad. That sounded like a put down to me. After all, where I was from, I was considered an adult at the age of sixteen. And I wondered how he knew I was from Overton Mills.

"I didn't mean anything by it," he said. "It's just that where I'm from, that's the way we refer to young lads. I know you're not a wee lad now. I just thought you must have learned to swim when you were a young lad. That's all."

"Yeah, yeah, I can swim," I said. I knew I shouldn't have answered him in that way, especially if he was sent by the creator of the universe, but after sitting on that hard cold ledge for who knew how long, I thought the creator of the universe could have sent him a little sooner.

I was tired and stiff and I knew my mood wasn't the greatest as I stood up and rubbed my sore butt. And it irritated me that I hadn't thought about swimming off this ledge myself after I realized I was in water. But I guess I was so terrified when I saw how far up I was that, that thought never crossed my mind.

Anyway, after this strange voice asked if I could swim, and I realized that I didn't have to hold my breath, I dove headfirst right off the cliff that I thought was my life line. I was amazed that I could swim with the same ease as the little fish around me. I swam up and down this large, dark cave as I darted in and out of all the little crevasses, exploring my new surroundings. I inspected the colorful glass-like crystals, which gave off that soft glow of diffused light that enabled me to see how vast this cavern actually was. I also examined white clusters of coral with razor sharp edges, as those little glowing fish that I had seen earlier darted in and out and all around their flower-like shapes. And then, beneath a clump of seaweed on the chamber's floor, I could see some tiny shrimp bouncing their way in and out as they scavenged for food.

But most of this vast cavern was dark and cold very unwelcoming.

Upon closer examination, as I swam around the cave's perimeter, I realized there were several tunnels leading to…who knew where? And I wasn't sure which one would lead me out.

Again came the voice of my new guide. "Lancer, are you coming out or not?"

"Yeah, I'm trying," I yelled. "Keep talking to me. I don't know which tunnel to take to get out. Maybe by following your voice, I will find the right one."

"Okay, my young lad," he said, making sure he didn't call me a wee lad again. "Just follow my voice." And at that, this strange new guide began singing in a muffled, yet enthusiastic, playful, bubbly voice. He sang, "Come follow me, my Lancer boy. Come follow me today. Come follow me, my Lancer boy. There is much I want to say."

Just listening to the funny, bubbly words coming from my new friend kind of made me chuckle. And as I followed his whimsical singing, I came to a small opening, about three feet tall and two and a half feet wide, at the base the cave wall. I carefully maneuvered through the small opening, taking care not to get snagged on some very sharp, jagged rocks that hung down on either side of my exit. When I finally got free from the cave, a whole new wondrous world appeared before me. It was a world of such vast beauty that it would normally have taken my breath away, but since I was underwater, I wasn't breathing anyway.

The water was filled with a multitude of sea life. I saw magnificent specimens of corals, in every color imaginable. I also saw many different kinds of seaweed, from plankton to kelp to specimens I'd never seen before, and they waved their long tentacle-like leaves in the mild underwater currents. And tiny black and white striped fish swam in and out of their foliage, feeding on the tiny organisms that had attached themselves to the plants outer sides. I also noticed several hermit crabs scurrying sideways across the sea floor, carrying their shell houses on their backs.

"Wow! This is great," I thought. But where had that voice, come from that led me out of the cave? As I looked around, I didn't see anyone. I swam around to the other side of the cave, but still I didn't see anyone.

"Mr. Thaumas," I called. "Where are you?"

Then came a hearty laugh behind me, accompanied by a torrent of bubbles that whizzed past me. This caused a slight wave that rocked me up and down. I quickly spun around to see who was there. And again I didn't see anyone. I only saw the tail end of what looked like a large gray dolphin swimming around a large mound of coral and seaweed. Again I called out, "Mr. Thaumas, where are you?"

Then, to my complete surprise, that large gray bottlenose dolphin that I had seen just minutes ago reappeared and gave me a wink as he quickly swam by, causing me to bounce up and down in the strong current, like I was nothing more than a large bobber on the end of someone's fishing line.

"No it couldn't be," I said as I saw him turn around to swim back to me.

"Why not?" came the joyful reply right from the long narrow mouth of this magnificent mammal. "I can clearly see now that you are definitely not a wee lad," he said playfully. And then he swam under me and lifted me with his hard but smooth muscular body and tossed me playfully over his back into a large clump of soft seaweed.

As I sat there trying to regain some sense of equilibrium, the dolphin swam right up to me and spoke again. "Why do you think it is so strange that I can speak to you? Didn't Lord Aster tell you that all things are possible? My, how one forgets so quickly." He held out a fin to help me up.

"Yeah, I guess he did, but I thought he meant within reason," I said.

"Did you think it reasonable to be tiny enough to be in a worm hole? Or to be the size of an ant?"

"Well, I hadn't given that much thought," I said, trying to keep him in sight as he swam up and down and all around me. "But at least the ants didn't talk to me."

"They might have if you had tried to talk to them first."

That was true. I hadn't tried to talk to them, but who would have thought that an ant could talk, and why would I want to talk to them anyway? Hmm. My mind was whirling again. This was so incredibly strange. I mean, here I was talking to a dolphin, and I didn't even need air to breathe. I was having a hard time wrapping my mind around everything. So I figured that it would be best just to accept it all, even though it didn't make a lick of sense to me. "Okay, I guess I will have to accept all of this, since here we both are, and you are definitely talking to me. So what's next?"

"Follow me," Thaumas said. "I want to show you this wonderful world, which is a part of the world you are from that most people will never have the opportunity to see."

So off we went. I followed Thaumas over cliffs and through hollowed-out rocks. We swam deep into dark crevasses and explored several underwater caves that weren't quite as large as the one I first found myself in. Then we swam near the sea's surface, and I could see an assortment of sea birds flying just above the mild waves. We stayed there for a while and watched the birds as they dove deep below the surface to catch fish that were swimming in large schools next to us and take back to their nests.

"Hey, Lancer my boy, you want to have a race?" Thaumas asked.

"Sure, but where are we going to race too?"

"There is an old ship that sunk many, many years ago, about a mile straight ahead. I bet I can beat you there."

Finally I felt like I had gotten my sea legs, so to speak, so I felt quite sure I could at least keep up with him and maybe even beat him. "Okay," I said. "Get on your mark, get set…" But before I could get the word *go* out, Thaumas had taken off. So off I went too.

We swam through many colorful school of fish and up and round several underwater mountains, but on dry land they would be considered foothills.

I was having a wonderful time. The sights were beautiful. At times I was ahead of Thaumas, and other times he was in front of me. I thought how wonderful it would be to actually be a fish and get this fanciful, fun life forever.

I saw the most fascinating things. There were all different kinds of jellyfish, starfish, and angelfish. There were fish that laid flat on the bottom of the sea with two eyes on the top looking straight up. There were octopuses, sea horses, stingrays, and giant turtles. And I thought how lucky they all were to have been created to live in such a beautiful place all the time.

Then, just after topping a small hill, we could see, settled in an ocean valley, the wreckage of an old ship that had sunk hundreds of years ago. As we got closer, I could see many pieces of gold and other treasures that had spilled to the ocean's floor from a place where the ship had broken in half. I wasn't sure if it had broken in half because of a battle of some kind or because age and rot from being in the ocean so long. It looked like an old pirate ship, with a carving of a skull and crossbones on its bow. This was truly a magical place. Any boy my age would have loved to hang out here with his friends and imagine being pirates searching for treasure.

Then, without warning, a large number of sharks appeared out of nowhere. I had never seen so many sharks in one place before and never so up close and personal!

They were thrashing the water and swimming erratically back and forth. There were hammerheads, great whites, tiger sharks, thresher sharks, and blue sharks. There were sharks unfamiliar to me, and they were all in a fierce feeding frenzy, biting at anything and everything in their way.

Terrified, I screamed, and a torrent of bubbles blasted from my mouth. "Thaumas, what should we do? Where can we go?"

"Into the ship," he yelled. "Hurry, Lancer, hurry!"

So as fast as I could, I shot like a harpoon straight for the ship, leaving a trail of bubbles and a current of waves behind me, and Mr. Thaumas was right on my tail, so to speak. We swam through a large hole on the front half of the ship for our dear lives.

Once we felt we were in relative safety we peered out of a small porthole in the bow of the ship and watched in horror as the sharks, in their bloodthirsty feeding frenzy, feasted on all the smaller fish that had been swimming around happily just minutes before. I don't really know if Thaumas was as frightened as me, but the thought of being a fish in this beautiful wonderland had vanished just as fast as it had come, after witnessing this blood thirsty massacre.

I again I thought of my parents and my friends and I wished I was home with them, as I clung to the old rotten wood of the ship's hull. As the thrashing continued just outside this rotting pirate ship we were hiding in, I closed my eyes and prayed for this madness to end. My heart raced, and my body shook with fear.

Chapter 11

The Human Organism

When I finally opened my eyes, I had again been transported to an unfamiliar place, and before me stood a small figure resembling a little girl of about six or seven years old. Her shiny black hair was pulled back into a ponytail with a pink ribbon, and she had the longest eyelashes I'd ever seen, which highlighted her beautiful green eyes. She was wearing a frilly white dress with puffy short sleeves and had a pink sash around her waist that matched the ribbon in her hair. Her shoes were also white, with pink shoelaces. And I wondered what this tiny girl could possibly teach me.

"Hello, my son," she said to me in a sweet but mature voice.

"My son! I'm not your son. You're not old enough to be anyone's mother," I said.

"Oh, but you are wrong, my dear young Lancer. I've been a mother to many, and you mustn't let looks deceive you. You see, I am very wise, and I am known as Shakti, which actually means life force energy. I am the life force that is in everything that has ever been created. And I am going to take you on a journey through one of my greatest creations now, my son."

Suddenly I realized that we were in a clear, colorless, round bubble, which was floating in a long, off-white transparent tube that appeared to have black markings down one side.

"What we are in, Shakti?" I asked, not so much out of fear but curiosity? Because by now I was beginning to realize that all these adventures were for me to learn some lesson. I needed to know what life was like from the perspective of many different creatures, I surmised. And I always managed to emerge unscathed from the experience.

"We are in a hypodermic needle, my son," she said. "And you are going to get to explore one of the greatest creations that was ever made—the human body. And, my child, you are going to get to view it from the inside. I am giving you the opportunity to see things that most people have never seen before and probably never will."

Then, before I had a chance to respond to this shocking revelation, I could feel someone picking up the hypodermic needle. It rocked our little bubble back and forth, knocking me off balance. Then I saw, to my horror, the plunger of the needle, which had been behind me all the time, coming straight for us. It pushed the liquid and our bubble into a human body. Now my curiosity was gone, and fear returned. The next thing I knew, we had been plunged into a stream of blue liquid, coursing through the veins of a human body.

"What is this blue river we are floating on?" I asked Shakti, trying not to show too much fear to this little girl.

"This is blood, my dear Lancer. This human that we are in has an infection, and he was given a shot of antibiotics to fight off the infection. We just hitched a ride in the needle so you could see how the human body works and how it fights off bad antibodies that weaken it."

"But I thought blood was red. This river is blue."

"My darling child, all blood is actually blue while it is in a body. It only turns red when it is exposed to air," she said. You see, the chemicals in air, when mixed with the chemicals of blood, alter it, thus changing its color."

"I'm not sure I can handle someone who looks younger than me calling me darling child," I said. "And if you are a mother, why do you look so young?"

"I can come to you as any form, sweet Lancer, but I decided this form would be less intimidating for you, especially given the voyage I'm taking you on. I knew you wouldn't let yourself be too afraid in front of a young girl. Don't you like this form?"

"Yeah, I guess so, but it's a little hard to take in, you know? Being called a child by a child."

"Well, my young Lancer, it is more important for you to pay attention to what I say and what you see around you than to get too caught up in my appearance."

"Okay," I said. "I'll try."

As we floated along in this blue river of blood, being jostled slightly back and forth continuously, I began to feel a bit queasy, knowing that I was actually in someone's body and not just floating along on a nice, sweet little boat ride. Was I ready for all this?"

Like Lord Aster, Shakti must have been able to read my thoughts and communicate telepathically, because I heard her voice in my mind without her actually talking to me. She said, "Yes, Lancer, you are ready for all of these experiences or you would not be going through them at this time. You see, my child, you have had many lifetimes to prepare for this moment in your spiritual evolvement. And the other masters and I believe that you are ready to see the workings of every part of this magnificent universe and its inhabitants for the work that we are preparing you to do."

Now I was really getting worried! To think that I must do a job so great that I had to know the workings of the universe and everything in it! After all, who was I to do a job that great? I was just a kid who went out for a joy ride one day with my best friend in my new Hydro Hover Machine. If I hadn't crashed, I wouldn't even be here at all. I was sure I wasn't ready for all this. They must have made a mistake. I could feel my skin getting all sweaty from the worry that I might be thrown into something that was just too big for me to do.

Then I felt Shakti touch my arm and saw her give me a reassuring smile. She said, "You will be ready, my son, before your first assignment, so you needn't worry."

As I looked around from the safety of our little bubble, I could see many other blue streams of blood flowing in all different directions. Some were parallel to the stream we were on, only going in the opposite direction, and others looked like little tributaries veering off in all directions. Then, suddenly, our little stream began to twist and turn back and forth, and I was being tossed from one side of our bubble to the other. It seemed as if we had entered a mighty river, with lots of rapids and many turns and bends. I saw large, strange clumps of debris that had no discernable shape to allow me to identify what they were. They were flowing rapidly by us as our little bubble ascended higher and higher through this human body.

"Where are we exactly, Shakti?" I asked. "I...I mean, where in the body are we?" I was stuttering because of being jostled so much.

"We are in the lower torso going up through the small intestines. And it won't be long before we enter the stomach. There you will see some real action, because this human is almost done eating his lunch, and then he will take a nap so the nutrients from his food and the antibiotic can go to work to help heal his body."

After traveling back and forth and around and around for some time in our little protective bubble, we entered a big tube that I could see opened up to a large cavity that was brimming with activity. "Is that the stomach?" I asked.

"Yes, dear Lancer. We are just beginning to enter it, so pay attention, and watch how food is digested in the human body. Oh, and brace yourself, because this is going to rock our little boat a bit." She gave me a little mischievous giggle, knowing that this was really going to do more than just rock our little boat.

The stomach cavity was half full of a green, murky, churning, sizzling liquid. It reminded me of my mom's split pea soup boiling on the stove. Then, all of a sudden, a very large glob of something—I suppose it was food—dropped from an opening just above us into this green volcanic stew. This caused a huge wave that spun our little bubble all around and knocked our little vessel into that churning soup.

I tried to brace myself, with both of my arms extended, pressing my palms against the interior walls of our little bubble. I could see the acidy green mixture of digestive enzymes dissolving that clump of food right before my eyes. We were no longer in our safe little blood vessel, because that big glob of food had caused a rupture in the stomach wall, depositing us right into the boiling pot!

"We're going to be boiled alive, I screamed as our little safe haven was being tossed from right to left and up and down. This pool of bubbling green goo sucked us down into its depths and spit us out over and over, trying to penetrate and dissolve our little force field.

"You're safe in here," said Shakti, using the same words Lord Aster had. "I think you've had enough of this experience, haven't you my child? Shall we be on our way?"

"Yes, I have. Please get us out of here."

Finally we left the stomach, and to my great relief we were floating calmly back on the blue river in another blood vessel. I knew I didn't need to ask how we got here, because I knew Shakti could do anything. And I was just happy to be out of the stomach.

"Where are we now?" I asked.

"We are about to enter one of the lungs."

It was nice to be out of the stomach, where there was such intense heat and constant battering about every time something new was swallowed. To be honest, I wasn't sure if I could have taken much more of that. But now, as we entered the lung, we had a new problem. Every time this human took a breath, it sounded like a freight train coming in and just about running us over before he exhaled and pushed the air out again. The noise was so loud that I wasn't sure my little eardrums would be able to take it much longer. So I put my hands over my ears and stared out of our little bubble in amazement to see how large the lung could expand. The lung was like a giant cave, which had countless tunnels that branched off like a huge tree with thousands of branches that fingered off in every direction. And the farther in we got, the more narrow these tunnels got.

I also noticed that when this human exhaled, his lung contracted so tightly that I was afraid we would be crushed from its deflation. The walls of the lung tributary we were in deflated so tight that it literally pressed in on all sides of our little bubble.

Then we entered into big cavity, and I noticed all these red and white blobs of various sizes and shapes racing in and attacking this very large black mass, which was blocking off some of the tunnels in this man's lung. "What are they, Shakti?" I asked while pointing at all those red and white blobs.

"Those are the red and white corpuscles sent by the brain to fight off that black mass you see over there. That mass is the infection I told you this person had. Watch closely, my son, and witness the marvel of the human body at work."

As I watched, I was amazed to see how the body used these corpuscles. They attached themselves to the infection and then dissolved it, just like the stomach acid dissolved the food. I marveled at how great God was to make such a body that knows how to heal itself.

"Thank you, Lancer," Shakti said.

At first it didn't dawn on me that she was acknowledging that she was God by thanking me for that thought, but when I looked at her for conformation, she just stared out of our translucent bubble and acted as though she had never said a thing.

After leaving the lung and giving my ears some much needed rest, Shakti again instructed me to brace myself. "We are now about to enter the heart," she said as she pointed in the direction that she wanted me to focus my attention."

I could feel and hear the soft, repetitive beat of the heart as we came ever nearer to the great life-giving organ of this magnificent human body.

Shakti had told me to brace myself, so I flattened myself as well as I could against the side of our transparent globe and braced my feet by locking my knees, but I spread my feet as far apart as I comfortable could, and I flattened my palms against each side of the bubble with my arms outstretched.

As I looked ahead, I saw a large, bluish-white oval organ drawing us to it with every beat, as it grew increasing louder. For a second I had forgotten that Shakti had told me that blood was naturally blue, but when I remembered I realized that this great pounding organ was the heart. The tremendous vibration on our little bubble threw us back and forth with such force that no amount of bracing did any good, and my poor little body was tossed mercilessly back and forth and all around.

And to make matters worse for me, that tremendous beating sound was so deafening that I thought I would go crazy as the heart muscle continued its rhythmic beat, drawing us ever deep within its chambers.

I didn't know how much more of this constant barrage, of being thrown around like a rag doll I could take. All I could think of was that I couldn't wait to get out of this organ, no matter how marvelous it was. And what about Shakti? Was she also flying around this orb like me? When I concentrated on finding her in this crazy ride, I noticed to my amazement that she wasn't being thrown around at all. She was just floating peacefully in the center of our little globe and acting as if nothing out of the ordinary was happening. The trashing of our transparent vehicle had no effect on her whatsoever!

Finally, the pounding grew less as we found our way out of the heart muscle and floated more calmly up through the neck on our way to the face.

After having had a chance to rest a little and quiet the rattling in my brain, I asked Shakti, "How come you didn't get thrown around our little globe like I did when we were traveling through the heart?"

"My dear son, remember your lessons. All things are possible with the power of thought. If you think of yourself as still and quiet in the mist of turbulence, and you have faith in that belief, then you will be still and quiet. That's all I did, my child. I can remain calm in any circumstance, and you can too if you remember your lessons and rely on what you've been taught."

She made it sound so simple, but could it actually be that simple? From that point on, I vowed to myself that the next time I found myself thrust into a situation that I felt was out of my control, I would try out my own power of thought and see if it worked for me like it did for her. After all, Lord Aster and Shakti both said I could do it, so it must have been true! All I needed was a little faith in myself, and how hard could that be?

Now, as we continued on our journey up the neck and into the face of this human, the ride became steady and smooth. The gentle swaying was so calming that I nearly fell asleep, but then I felt the soft nudging from this young, powerful girl called Shakti as she told me she didn't want me to miss anything. So I made myself stretch to shake the fatigue from my body and tried to stay alert as we steadily moved forward on our human journey.

As our little bubble continued to ride the bloodstream up through the nose and into the eye, I was amazed that I could now see the same things this man could see. I saw the room he was in and all the furniture. I could see a window and the trees outside. Excited, I almost yelled, "Shakti, Shakti. How can I be seeing the room this man is in and his window and the outside?"

"Calm down, sweet Lancer. The reason you can see what this man sees is because we are passing through his iris, and the iris is like a mirror which reflects what this room looks like to the back of this man's brain, where it is then processed. We, dear Lancer, are seeing that reflection as this information bounces back to us before going to the brain center, where it is recorded for all time.

"Oh, so we're just seeing a reflection of this man's room and not the actual room—like a mirror?"

"Yes, my child, you got it. Now let's move on."

Just as I was getting comfortable again and resting nicely as we traveled in a smooth uninterrupted bliss, it suddenly became extremely bright, almost blindingly bright! "What's that light?" I said as I covered my eyes with both hands, just peering through a small crack between two open fingers.

"We have just entered the spiritual eye, between the eyebrows."

"Spiritual eye? What's that?"

"This is the place known as the eye of perception, where ideas are formed and all material things can be made manifest. First comes the idea, and then the way to create it. This is where all creative thinkers focus their attention when they want to solve a problem or create something they desire."

"But why is it so bright?" I asked?

"I'm sure you have seen comic strips in your newspapers or a comic book in which they show an individual with a bright light bulb above his or her head, signifying that they just got an idea, haven't you? Well, there truly is a spiritual light in your mind, also known as your mind's eye, and it is located just above and between the eyebrows at the forward part of your head." She pointed with her finger to a spot on my forehead. "Lord Aster told you a bit about meditation. Do you remember?" she asked.

"Yes, I remember. He told me to sit with my back straight and concentrate on something good, like love, peace, or strength, but he said I should never concentrate on anything negative." I spoke with glee, remembering what he'd told me.

"Yes, that's right, my child, but you must also focus your concentration at the point between your eyebrows, which is your spiritual eye. This is the area that can bring your thoughts to fruition or manifestation, my dear one."

Slowly, as my eyes became accustomed to the extreme light, I began to see images forming all around our bubble. There were pictures of buildings and skyscrapers, and then there were many numbers floating around us. Then I saw large sheets of paper, which looked like blueprints or drawings. I also saw various tools, like slide rules and hammers and saws and construction workers, and everything seemed a jumbled mess.

"What's going on now?" I asked.

"My dear Lancer, this person is thinking about his job. He's an architect, and he has much to do for his new project. His mind is thinking of the new office building that he's been hired to design, so he's thinking of everything he needs in order to make his plans come to life. He's figuring the dimensions for the building. Those are the numbers you see floating all around you. This man will use these numbers in order to create the blueprints for those building he's going to design. He also knows that he will need to hire a construction crew, and he sees in his mind the kinds of tools they will use to get the job done. All of these pictures that you see are actually thoughts that have been manifest first in his mind's eye before he can bring them to life on paper, and once the design has been put on paper, it can be built by the construction crew he hires. This is one way the mind works to bring material things into existence, but when the mind is powerful enough, it will be able to bring any material thing into existence just by the power of thought."

"Wow! This is all so amazing! Does everyone have this spiritual eye, or eye of perception, between their eyebrows?"

"Yes, dear Lancer; however, most people don't really use it well. They haven't learned how to fully concentrate at this spot to bring their desires into reality, but in time, everyone will come to that point in their evolution when they too can tap into to this form of concentration.

Now we were entering the brain, and I began to notice that it was like we had entered a great electrical storm. Lightning flashes came in great torrents of electrical currents all around us.

There was nowhere we could look that wasn't being illuminated by the powerful currents of white flashes that surged through the pulsating activity of this man's brain as it was being triggered by thoughts and other stimuli from his body.

I never imagined there was so much activity going on in a human brain before, and I wondered if this kind of activity was going on in my own brain right now?

"Yes, indeed, my child," said Shakti to my unvoiced question. "Even in your sleep, my son, there is a storm of activity going on in your mind, which keeps your body working as it should even without your knowledge of it."

As we continued to travel through the brain, I could tell we were ascending to the top of the head, and I asked, "Shakti, where will we go once we get to the top of this person's head? I mean, is that a way out, or will we have to go back through the body again?"

"The top of the head is where the crown chakra is located, my dear Lancer," she said. "It is at this point that a person, through strict adherence to spiritual practices, is able to transcend duality and become whole, or one with the universe; however, my dear child, you must still experience much and learn more before you can reach that level. So, dear son, once we start to ascend into that area, you will become increasingly tired and will drift off into a deep and renewing sleep, and when you awake, you will be at your next destination in your spiritual journey."

Even before she stopped telling me what to expect, I could feel my eyes getting heavy and my body going limp as my muscles relaxed. I felt a calming sense of peace, and all worries lifted. I fell into a total state of unconsciousness as we entered this man's crown chakra.

Chapter 12

The Funeral

My next conscious awareness was of a cool, gentle mist on my face, urging me to open my eyes. After looking around a bit, I realized I was standing in a cemetery next to a freshly dug grave, and I wondered why I would be set down in a place like this.

I scoured the landscape for my next spirit guide, hoping to learn why I was here. And as I looked around I saw a large black hover hearse descending into the cemetery parking lot, followed by a long stretch hover limousine that landed directly behind the hearse. After that came a procession of civilian hover machines in all shapes, sizes, and colors. They were being directed to specific parking spots, by several Overton Mills policeman. I knew they were Overton Mills policeman because I recognized their city logo on the side of their hover machines.

As I curiously watched this scene unfold, I wondered why on earth I was here. I couldn't imagine what I could possibly learn from being in a cemetery, but instinctively, I knew there must be a good reason, or I wouldn't have been sent here.

Just then, two men stepped from the hearse. They methodically moved to the back of the vehicle, as if they were soldiers on a mission, and opened the rear door. Together they drew out a rather plain looking casket. There was nothing special that would suggest such precision on the part of those two fellows, but nonetheless, they cared for that casket like their life depended on it.

I then glanced back at the limo to see who had lost their loved one, and what I saw left me dumbfounded. My own parents and paternal grandparents stepped from the limo. Mr. and Mrs. Byron Puckett were my dad's parents, but my mom's parents had long passed, so they weren't with them. Who in heavens name had they come to say good-bye to? I didn't have any brothers or sisters to bury, and my parents had no siblings either, so it couldn't have been a family member who'd recently died. I wondered whom they had come to morn on this drizzly, gray day.

Then to my surprise I saw several of my school buddies: Jeremy Livingston, Cameron Lutz, Canyon Cruz, and my best friend, Jake Merlot, picked up the casket behind the hover hearse and carried it to the open grave next to where I had been standing just moments ago. They gently place it evenly on the support braces that suspended it over the grave.

I looked back to find my dad with his right arm around Mom's shoulder as he gently grasp her left elbow with his left hand to help her descend the slippery hill leading to the grave site. Grandma and Grandpa Puckett followed close behind, also trying not to slip on the wet grass.

I was sure they would see me and wonder where I'd been all this time. Franticly, I waved my arms and called out their names. "Mom, Dad, I'm over here!" But as they drew nearer, they just kept their eyes on the ground, watching every step they made so they wouldn't slip and fall.

I thought it might be better if I waited until they were seated to get their attention. That way I wouldn't startle them and cause an accident.

Once they reached the casket, Mom dabbed her nose with a lace handkerchief and laid a single yellow rose in the center of the plain brown box. Again I wondered who could be so important in that box that my own parents didn't even notice me or hear me when I had called out to them.

Our family priest, Father Jacob, then escorted my parents and grandparents to sit in the first four folding chairs positioned on the front row next to the casket. Taped to the back of each of those four chairs were big yellow bows, but all of the other chairs were just plain gray folding chairs. This told me that whoever was in the casket was someone very special to my family, since they were the ones seated in those special chairs. But for the life of me, I just couldn't figure out who it could possibly be.

Confused and worried, I tried to get Mom and Dad's attention again. "Mom, Dad, I'm right here. Don't you see me?" I said as I squatted before them and waved my hand in front of their faces?" Still they took no notice of me and just sat there sobbing quietly as they waited for the funeral to begin.

Desperate to get someone's attention, I walked over to Jake and waved my hands in front of him, saying, "Hey, buddy, don't you see me? It's me, Lance. Please say something!"

But sadly, Jake took no notice of me either. Now I was really freaked out. Why couldn't anyone see me? What was going on? Nothing made any sense to me. And I wanted some answers. No! I needed some answers and I needed them now!

Then Father Jacob stood up and began speaking. The words he started off with totally blew me away. He said, "We come here today to honor and say good-bye to our beloved son, grandchild, friend, and companion, Lancer Puckett, who died in the prime of his life on his sixteenth birthday in a terrible accident in his new Hydro Hover Machine."

"What? No! This is impossible," I screamed. "I can't be dead. I remember Estrella telling me that I wasn't dead. Surely she wouldn't lie to me. This is all a terrible nightmare." I paced nervously back and forth between my parents and the casket as the priest continued to ramble on about how much I would be missed and what a good boy I had been.

Then I remembered the crash, and all the experiences I'd had since then came flooding back to me. "Yes, I must be dead," I said out loud, knowing no one could hear me.

As the funeral concluded the mist had now turned into rain and everyone was hurrying to their respective vehicles to leave the cemetery. I ran after Mom and Dad, yelling as loud as I could to get their attention one more time, but as before, they acted as if they couldn't hear me. I tried to grab Dad's arm, but my hand went right through it, and they just kept going. They got back in the limo, and it flew off.

Grief stricken and defeated, I walked back to the grave and sat on the wet grass, and I watched two cemetery attendants lower the plain brown wooden box into the ground. Then a third man, in a bulldozer, dumped a shovel full of dirt over the casket. I must have sat there next to my own grave for hours in a daze, hardly believing what I had just witnessed. Depressing thoughts bombarded my mind—thoughts like, if I was dead, really dead, then what was next? Was I just stuck here to watch everyone else enjoy life while I was suspended in some kind limbo, unable to interact with them? I thought if there truly is a hell, this surly was it!

Chapter 13

Meeting Doshi Tow: Spirit Guide Number 3

The rain hadn't let up one bit since everyone had deserted the cemetery hours earlier, which just added to the forlorn feeling I had in the pit of my stomach. My heart felt like it was broke beyond repair. I raised my head to cool my face in the rain and rinse the stinging tears from my eyes. Just then, I happened to notice a boy about my age coming toward me. His hair was coal black, and I could tell from his complexion and eyes that he was of Asian descent.

At first I thought nothing of it. I figured he was just someone coming to pay his respects to a loved one. But then I wondered why on earth he would come out here on such a dismal rainy day. Why wouldn't he have waited until the rain had stopped?

Just as I decided it was none of my business and was about to turn away, this strange kid started running toward me, waving his hand and smiling in a friendly gesture, as if to say hello.

At first I didn't know what to think. I didn't know this kid was from Adam, so why was he running toward me? Did he know me? Did he come to tell me to leave?

"Hello, Lancer. My name is Doshi Tow," he enthusiastically announced. "Do you like sitting in the rain?"

"No, not really," I said, wondering why he would ask such an obvious question when he saw how wet and miserable I looked.

"Then come with me," he said. "I know a place to dry off and get something good and warm to eat. You'll feel a lot better. I can guarantee it." Doshi Tow gave me a friendly slap on the back."

Wiping the wet hair from my eyes, I looked up at this strange new kid. "Are you my next spirit guide?" I figured he must be, because he could see me and talk to me and even touch me, or should I say slap me, when all the other people I saw that day couldn't.

"Yes, I am," he said. "I bet you probably think I'm kinda young to be a spirit guide, don't you?"

"I hadn't really given it much thought," I said. "But now that you mention it, the answer is no, not at all, because I had a spirit guide who was younger than you called Shakti. She was just a little girl."

"Oh, that's right," Doshi Tow said. "But she's not really that young. In fact, she doesn't even really have an age. But I, on the other hand, I am young, so to speak." He patted himself in the chest with both hands. "But don't get me wrong. I've been around many, many lifetimes, and that has given me plenty of time to learn what I needed to in order to become a spirit guide." He had a big grin on his face. "It's just that I crossed over to this realm when I was sixteen, like you, and I decided to keep my youthful look. And by the time you've gone through all of your training like I have, you may be one too." He offered his hand to help me up.

I wondered what kind of training I would have to go through. And what did he mean, exactly, when he said I might be a spirit guide? I also wondered what the duties of a spirit guide were. Did they just help people who had passed on to assimilate into this strange spirit world that I had entered to?

"I have a feeling we are going to be very good friends, Lance my boy. By the time you are ready to take your place in the universal plan, we will know each other very well indeed," Doshi Tow said with a tone of certainty.

"What is my place in the universal plan?"

"Well, Lance…you don't mind if I call you Lance, do you? I mean since we are going to be good friends, I figured it would be all right if I called you a more familiar name, like a nick name, instead of Lancer, which is kinda formal, if you ask me. And you can call me Doshi."

"Yeah, I guess it's okay if you call me that," I said. "But, what about my question? What is my role in the universal plan?"

"Well, Lance, everyone has different roles and different things they must learn and experience, and I can't really say for sure what your role will be until after we have our group meeting and I have had a chance to consult with the other guides."

Doshi then led me around the back of a large tombstone, and he appeared to open an invisible door. The rain was coming down much harder now, and my clothes were clinging to me, sending shivers up and down my body, from the bottom of my feet to the top of my head.

"Aren't you going in to get out of the rain?" Doshi asked me as he motioned with his hand to go forward.

"What do you mean, out of the rain?" I said, looking around this cold bleak cemetery. I couldn't see any place to go to get out of the rain except a building that was about a mile down the road behind us. And he was directing me to go forward through a door that wasn't there. I thought he was just playing around, when all of a sudden, he gave me a powerful shove from behind, and I fell face first to the ground through the invisible door that he had just opened into a cemetery identical to the one we were in. The only difference was that this one was warm, sunny, and dry. There wasn't a cloud in the sky.

Doshi Tow quickly stepped in after me and pulled the invisible door closed, and I heard it latch shut.

"Wow! What just happened?" I asked. My mind was whirling from this new experience. "How did it stop raining so fast? And look—our clothes are already dry." As I looked around, I noticed that nothing on me or around me was the least bit wet. The sun was warm, and it was just getting to be midafternoon. And I was surprised to see that everything looked so much more alive than I'd remembered. All the flowers next to the graves in this cemetery were beautiful and smelled so wonderful. I couldn't believe just minutes ago, Doshi Tow and I were in a downpour in this very same cemetery. Or was it the same cemetery? I wasn't sure.

"Doshi, please explain what just happened to us. How can everything be so warm and dry and beautiful now, when just a minute ago I was standing in a downpour and shivering all the way to my bones?"

"We just stepped into an alternate dimension. This is still your world and still your time, but it is a different dimension. This dimension is your next classroom to help you develop your consciousness." Doshi Tow was very nonchalantly.

Questions were coming so fast that they were piling up, and I couldn't decide which one to ask first, but I finally managed to form one question that had been bothering me for some time now. "Doshi Tow, I had a spirit guide named Estrella, and she told me that I wasn't dead, yet I just came from my own funeral. How can that be? Was she lying to me? Am I really dead or not?"

"Lance, please call me Doshi," he said again with a playful smile. He motioned for us to go toward a soft patch of grass beneath a large oak tree next to a sizable marble mausoleum. Please sit, and I will try to answer some of your questions."

So I sat with my long legs outstretched and my back comfortably up against the trunk of the large oak tree. I was ready to get some much needed relaxation time and have some of my questions answered.

Doshi sat down facing me, with his legs crossed like an Indian at a campfire. He then gave me a long yet thoughtful stare before he spoke. "The answer to your question is both yes and no." I gave him a quizzical stare before he continued. "Your physical body has certainly passed away. That is to say, it is now in a state of decomposition and there is no life force remaining in your body, except that which is needed to decompose the flesh and bones and return them to their original state of gasses and molecules. But, my dear Lance, the physical body was not you. It was never the real you. It was just a vehicle that you used while you lived in the physical world. You see, Lance, you have had many, many physical vehicles that the real you has used over many lifetimes to learn the necessary lessons it needed to learn to advance to a higher state of consciousness. You just didn't remember any of them, but your spirit, also known as your soul, did."

"Well, how can I learn anything if I can't remember any of my past lives?"

"That's a hard one for most people to understand," Doshi said. "But you needn't worry yourself about that, because your soul remembers everything, even if your physical brain can't. The subconscious mind is what some refer to as the soul, and that is the real you. The subconscious mind is a small part of the greater consciousness, also referred to as the super consciousness. This is the creator of all that ever was, is, and will be."

I was still confused, and it didn't seem possible that my subconscious mind could remember all my past lives when I couldn't.

Sensing that I was having a hard time believing all this, Doshi Tow gave an example of how the soul remembers. "Lance," he said, with an understanding tone to his voice. "Have you ever wondered why some people are afraid of heights or afraid to swim in water over their heads when nothing in this life has led them to be afraid of these things?"

Doshi answered his own question before I had a chance to. "It's because in a previous life, they may have fallen from a great height or drowned in a large body of water, and their subconscious mind remembers those events and cautions the individual to be wary or afraid so as to keep him from those dangers again. The individual doesn't need to remember the actual act that happened, because the real you does remember. But you see, young Lance, your subconscious mind is kind enough and wise enough to keep those memories from your conscious mind, because you would go crazy if you remembered everything from every lifetime you have ever lived. Why don't you rest awhile, Lance, and let all this sink in. I can tell that all of this information has tired you."

I agreed because it was an awful lot to take in at one time. So I closed my eyes to get some much needed rest.

Chapter 14

My New Friends

"Lance, Lance, get up. It's time to get up," Doshi said as he playfully ran a pointing stick up my side as if to tickle me to full consciousness. "You must get up now or we will be late." He nudged me a little harder with his foot to shake me awake.

"Late for what?"

"Our group meeting, Lancer. Don't you remember me telling you that we would have a group meeting?" he said as he held out his hand to help me to my feet.

"Yeah, I remember you saying something about talking to other guides before you could say if I would be a spirit guide or not."

"Yes, that's right, but at this group meeting, you will be meeting other kids just like you, who are also in training. They are all at the same level of development that you are at right now, Lance. And they have been informed that you are coming and are very anxious to meet you. Now come on!"

Others? Now my interest was really piqued. I couldn't wait to meet other kids just like me. I didn't know why, except that there was something within me that needed to know there were other kids who were also struggling with this new realm of existence. I wanted to know that I wasn't alone! So I hopped right up and said, "Okay, Doshi, let's go. I'm ready to meet these other people, so lead the way!"

Doshi could tell I was excited to go and meet some new friends, so he smiled broadly and bowed low before me (according to his custom) and said, "Of course, my dear boy. Let us go."

He then grabbed my hand, and up we went—up in the air! I felt like Peter Pan, a character from a nursery story my mother used to read to me when I was very young. I could feel the cool air on my face, which exhilarated and excited me, and I loved this feeling of freedom that I got from flying without even a hover machine or plane or anything at all except holding onto Doshi's hand. This was wonderful, and I wanted so much to learn to do this all by myself.

Soon we landed on a pristine white marble patio, next to a very large white building with no windows and no doors. The patio had four large white urns filled with the most beautiful dainty pink flowers and only a touch of green foliage to contrast with the little blooms, which gave off a beautiful aroma that could calm any soul. These urns had been placed on each corner of the patio, and long white marble benches were placed evenly between each planter. The building looked like a large plain box, about fifty feet tall, with no distinctive markings except for a few words carved into the top edge of the building. The words were in a language I couldn't understand, so I paid them no mind. But I did wonder what this large plain stone box was used for.

"Where are we, Doshi?" I said when he finally let go of my hand after we had landed.

"We are here at your new school," he said with a grin.

"My new school? Where is the door? How do we get in?"

Then, just like he had done in the cemetery, he gave me a slight push toward that large white box, and right through the wall I went. Once in, I recognized this chamber as the same place I found myself in when I woke up after my accident. Only this time, there was an extremely large table that stretched from where I had entered all the way down that endless corridor that I had seen Estrella emerge from when I had first met her. The table was filled with all kinds of savory foods that made my mouth water in anticipation, because I couldn't really remember the last time I had eaten. And on either side of the table, there were hundreds of chairs lined up for as long as I could see, filled with boys and girls about my age, talking and laughing and truly enjoying themselves. No one even seemed to notice that I had arrived, even after Doshi entered the chamber.

"Aren't you going to sit down and get acquainted?" Doshi asked as he motioned to the table.

"But where?" I said as looked around and didn't see any spare chairs.

Just then, Doshi went to the head of the table near, where we had entered, and rang a loud bell that had been sitting on a small side table next to the wall. The bell sounded more like a large gong than a simple bell, even though it was a small, plain, brass bell that looked like it would only make a slight ting-ting sound when rung. But the actual sound that came from that tiny bell was loud and deep, and it reverberated in my ears.

Immediately, every one stopped and gave Doshi their undivided attention.

"My dear sons and daughters, I would like to introduce our newest son to you. His name is Mr. Lancer Puckett, and he only just arrived today," he said.

Only just arrived today? Why, I'd been there a long time. I'd been through hell and back. I recalled all the adventures I had gone through. But I decided it would be better not to try to correct him at this time, in front of everyone. And I was still having a hard time seeing Doshi as a father figure, but I guess he was, because he called everyone sons and daughters.

"Please make him feel welcome," Doshi said.

Then everyone began clapping and cheering as they welcomed me to their group.

As I stood there feeling all embarrassed, I could feel the blood rush to my face, and I just knew that my cheeks were turning as red as ripe cherries. Just then I noticed the table seemed to expand in length right before my eyes, and another chair amazingly appeared near the head of the table. As I pulled the chair out to take a seat, another plate appeared in the spot right before me, filled with delicious-looking food, and a scrumptious aroma wafted up to my nose, making my mouth water with anticipation as hunger pains now reminded me that I hadn't eaten for a while. I was ready for a good meal.

"Hi, my name is Cory, Cory Romer," said the kid who was sitting to my left. He was about my height and weight, but his hair was the color of golden wheat, not blond like mine. He had a slight mustache and a patch of hair on his chin, which was supposed to be a goatee, I surmised. He held out his hand in a friendly greeting, and I happily accepted it and introduce myself to him.

He then brought my attention to the person sitting to my right and said, "I would like to introduce you to Miss Sheila Mizel."

When I turned to my right to greet this new person, I temporarily lost all composure. My hands got all sweaty, and I could feel my heart racing wildly in my chest. There! Right there, sitting next to me, was the most beautiful red-haired girl I'd ever seen in my entire life. She was extending her delicate hand in a gracious greeting, and before I could except her hand in mine, I had to wipe the sweat off on my jeans under the table to keep her from realizing just how nervous I was at meeting someone so utterly beautiful as she was.

She had gorgeous, long, curled eyelashes, which set her remarkable crystal blue eyes alight with a sparkle that seemed to draw me in. Her high cheekbones were rosy, and her full lips were as red as a pomegranate. Immediately, all thoughts of food vanished, and it seemed as if this beautiful creature and I were the only ones in the room.

A strange feeling of familiarity came over me. It was a feeling of some kind of deep, profound love. This love felt eternal. I felt like I had always known and always loved this beautiful girl. But how could I? I only just met her. I wondered what had caused this immense deep emotion within my heart. I could see that this girl was beautiful, but I had never had such a deep feeling for someone at first sight before.

After managing to dry my hand on my pant leg, I offered it to Sheila and said, "Hello, Miss Sheila Mizel." My voice cracked and trembled as I tried to get the words out.

She smiled so kindly at me and said, "It's a great pleasure to meet you, but it seems as though we've known each other forever, so please just call me Sheila."

Jolting me back to reality, Doshi said, "It's time to eat, so let's not let this good food go to waste. And after dinner, we will have a question and answer period before we assign you to your separate classes."

Once Doshi had finished speaking, everyone began to eat. No other words were spoken. I looked around at all the other kids, eating with such intense joy. The only sound that could be heard were the sounds of forks clinking on the plates as everyone scooped up their food, and then the rhythmic, soft sound of people chewing. I didn't know if this was some unwritten law—to eat in silence—but I decided I had better follow suit. So I too began eating.

The first bite was so incredibly flavorful and delicious that I couldn't wait for the next bite, as I shoved more and more food into my mouth.

No wonder no one spoke. Everyone's forks went from their plates to their mouths. Like me, I'm sure they didn't want to waste a moment between bites with unnecessary small talk.

When I briefly looked up, between bites, I noticed Doshi on one side of the room, visiting with several other people, all dressed in the same orange robes with black rope-like belts tied loosely around their waists. I just figured that they were the other guides that he had told me about earlier, since he was dressed as they were. So I just continued eating and enjoying every bite, as if it was a wonderful Thanksgiving dinner, because to me it was. Here I was with good friends and great food. What more could I ask for?

Chapter 15

Questions And Answers

When the last person had finished eating—which, as you can imagine, didn't take long since it was so delicious—several brilliant, light beings floated in to clear the table.

Then Doshi had us all take our chairs and put them in several rows of ten deep, one behind the other, for our question-and-answer session. While everyone was setting up their chairs as instructed, the light beings that had cleared the table were now pushing the tables in on themselves like a folding accordion door, down the long corridor until it vanished from sight.

I was very happy that Cory and Sheila had decided to sit next to me again, Cory on my left, and Sheila on my right. I truly hoped Sheila would want to become close friends with me, because I couldn't shake this feeling that we were meant to be together. And after our introduction at dinner and the strange, remarkable familiarity I felt for her, I sure didn't want to lose that friendship now.

Cory was very friendly too, and I thought the three of us would make a wonderful study team, helping each other figure out problems and sharing ideas. If that was how our classes were to be designed, so that students could help each other. I could only hope that the guides would place us in the same class.

As we sat there waiting for the question-and-answer segment to begin, I became aware that the room was buzzing with the soft sounds of everyone quietly chatting among themselves as they tried to remember all of the questions which had been haunting their minds since they had crossed over into this wonderfully strange and yet sometimes frightening world.

When I looked around, I saw that some people were writing their questions down on napkins that they had taken from the table before it was cleared, and others were comparing their experiences with the people next to them.

I wanted to turn to Sheila and ask her about the experiences she has had since she had crossed over, but I didn't want her to think I was being too personal, since we had only just met at dinner. However, just as I was about to get up the nerve to question her, Doshi rang that small copper bell again, and the loud reverberating sound of the gong immediately drew everyone's attention to the front of the room.

As I looked around, I didn't see the other people he had been talking to while we were eating, and I wondered where they had gone.

"Ladies and gentlemen," said Doshi. "Some of you have already met the other guides that I'm going to be introducing to you shortly; but some of you have not. They are of the highest order in the spiritual realm, but do not be intimidated, for they all started out as you are starting out now. They will arrive momentarily and will be happy to answer the questions that I know have filled your minds since you all crossed over to this dimension. Then, when the question-and-answer session is over, you will quietly and in an orderly manner go to the end of the corridor, where you will find several lists attached to the wall. These lists will tell you who your guide will be for the first semester and where your classes are located. Once you find out the name of your guide, you will go to that class for a short get-acquainted session. At the end of your meetings with your new guides they will tell you where your dorms are, and you will then be allowed to go and settle in and get more acquainted with your roommates before your first class begins. But now I would like to take this opportunity to introduce to you, with great pleasure, the other guides that will be helping you to advance in your spiritual evolution."

Excitedly, we all waited on the edge of our chairs to meet the other guides. Then three opalescent light forms slowly descended next to Doshi and materialized into Estrella, Lord Aster, and Shakti. Only this time, Shakti was not in the form of a little girl. She was a beautiful woman, with smooth, soft skin and long flowing onyx-black hair braided down to the middle of her slender waist. And even though she was dressed just like all the others, in an orange robe with a plain black rope belt loosely draped around her waist, I could tell it was Shakti by her beautiful face and lovely green eyes.

Doshi motioned to Lord Aster and introduced him. "I would like you to meet Lord Aster. He is also known as a Jnana Yogi. A Jnana Yogi is one who finds union with God through the discriminative power of the intellect and wisdom of the soul."

Then he directed our attention to Estrella and said, "This kind soul is Estrella, who is a Karma Yogi. A Karma Yogi is one who reaches union with God through selfless service for others. She has become free of the ego by this method and has merged with the one and only creator of the universe. And you all know me, as I have been with all of you at one time or another. I am a Bhakti Yogi. The Bhakti Yogi has achieved the universal oneness with super-consciousness through the spiritual approach of love and devotion.

"And last, but certainly not least, is Shakti." He waved his hand in her direction. "Shakti is the very essence of all that is! She is also referred to as Prana, which are the very sparks of intelligence, the finer-than-atomic energy that constitutes life itself." As Doshi spoke, you could hear the obvious sound of reverence in his voice and could tell that he held Shakti in high esteem.

As I looked at each of the guides standing before us, including Doshi Tow, I noticed a beautifully colored aura that encased each of their entire forms. These auras radiated a powerful energy that put me in a state of awe at their magnificence. And in the eyes of each of these spiritual giants, I could see an infinite channel of wisdom—a wisdom that could be tapped into if one had the know-how to pierce that great vat of infinite knowledge, which I had never noticed before.

Shakti spoke first. "Good day, my darling children. I'm sure there are many questions you would like to ask us, and now is the time that we will begin to answer some of them. But first, on your laps, each of you will find a small blank journal, which you can log your questions and answers in so that in the future you may refer to them when the need arises."

When I looked down on my lap, sure enough, there was a small, iridescent bluish-purple notebook. The words Lancer Puckett's Journal were printed on the front cover, and attached to journal with a silver cord was a matching pen to write with. As I thumbed through this thin book, which was no larger than the palm of my hand and would fit easily in a front pocket of any shirt, I noticed that each page was numbered, and the numbers went on and on and on. There seemed to be an infinite number of pages in this very small book, but what was so astonishing was that when the book was closed, it was no thicker than the pen that accompanied it.

Shakti said, "When you would like to ask one of us a question, all you need to do is hold up your pen." She illustrated with a pen of her own. "And the pen will turn colors, according to which one of us you wish to address your question to. For instance, if you have a question for Lord Aster and you hold up your pen, the pen will turn an ocean blue, and if you have a question for Estrella, your pen will turn a pastel pink, and if you have a question for Doshi, your pen will turn an emerald green, and if you have a question for me, your pen will turn a vibrant golden yellow."

As she was explaining all of this to us, her pen was changing colors to illustrate what our pens would look like when we had questions.

"Now, let's begin," she said.

The first question came from someone several rows behind us. "Please tell us, why do you have all those vibrant, colorful lights encircling all of you, and is it possible for us to have them too?"

The answer came from Estrella, so even though we couldn't see behind us, we knew that the pen that our fellow student held up was pastel pink.

Estrella said, "My dear Angelo, these luminous, shimmering bands of rainbow colors radiating from our bodies and encircling our forms are bands of radiant energy, also known as auras. This energy emanates from the highest plane of consciousness, entering and leaving our bodies through the chakras. These magnificent colors of energy are electromagnetic fields, which equip us with a superb sensitivity to external influences. This allows us to send our own energy vibrations into the world as we see necessary. And yes, my dear child, you already have an aura. Everyone does; however, not everyone has yet developed the ability to see this with the naked eye. You are blessed indeed to have evolved enough to see ours, and if you put your mind to it, you can see your own too."

"Wow," was the first thought that came to my mind after hearing Estrella's answer. This was only the first question, and already I was having a hard time getting everything that she had said down in my little journal.

Then Sheila raised her pen, and it turned an emerald green, so I knew her question was for Doshi. "What is this energy field, or aura, as Estrella called it, used for?"

Doshi Tow stepped forward to speak. "Everyone's aura is a complete physical, mental, emotional, and spiritual map of an individual's life and character. It shows us patterns of thought and the flow of physical and emotional energy of an individual. The aura can show us if a person is in need of a healing of some kind—be it physical, mental, or spiritual—or if they need to be energized due to lack of rest. It can also show us if an individual is malnourished or suffering from some emotional state such as fear or loneliness or sadness."

Another student wanted to know if the colors had any particular meaning. And this time, Lord Aster answered. "Yes indeed, my child. Red means you are vibrantly active. It also reveals physical energy or anger. Pink is a sign of unselfish love and sensitivity. This is the color of a practicing healer, or it may indicate that spiritual healing is currently being implemented. Orange is a sign of healthy sexuality. Muddy shades of this color mean self-indulgence. Yellow signifies intellect, warmth, and compassion. A muddy or dark yellow denotes a fearful, resentful, lazy person, who thinks the world owes him or her something. Gold is truly a spiritual color and is rarely seen in the aura. It is the sign of a saint or a godly being. Silver is a color that denotes an erratic mental energy and signifies that the person has a mental illness. Green shows balance and growth. Blue can be a deeply healing color, and it indicates an independent spirit. Depending on how deep the color is, it may show the person to be stubborn or dogmatic in his beliefs. Purple is the timeless color of the priest or priestess and is emanated by the seeker of truth. Gray or black bands of the aura over the head of a person show that he or she suffers depressed thoughts, and anywhere else on their body they mean that they harbor negative emotions or disease. Brown bands in an aura point to a materialistic person with good business skills. White, like gold, is not often seen in ones aura, but if it is there, then this indicates a highly evolved, divinely spiritual being."

My pen could hardly keep up as I tried to capture every answer, word for word. However, even though these had been good questions, my mind kept coming back to a question that I needed an answered to.

It stood to reason that if Shakti was the life force energy of all things, then she must have the answer to my particular question. So I slowly raised my pen, and it turned a vibrant golden yellow, indicating my question was for Shakti.

"Go ahead, Lancer my son," she said with the sweetest voice, which could only be compared to a loving mother cooing to her newborn baby.

I timidly asked, "What is the mind of God, and can we know it?"

Shakti glowed with a shimmering, brilliant golden hue, and the pools of molten wisdom churned in her all-knowing eyes as she began to answer. "All things, my son, from a single tiny organism in a small tide pool to the infinite number of massive universes, are all connected. Mathematical laws bind everything together. Inside every atom is a void, but it is not really a void, because this void is filled with pure consciousness. The human mind only uses four percent of the consciousness that your science has been able to measure, known as mind stuff, so the question is, how much more can we not see? How much more can we capture from the infinite universe? How much more are we able to know?"

She went on to say, "Thought particles are neutral, so we have to be in a neutral state to access our own subconscious world. Once you are able to access this subconscious world, it will lead you to the super-conscious mind, or in other words, to God. We have to be neither awake nor asleep. We have to be in a state of deep meditation to be fully aware. Once we are fully aware, we know that we are the mind of the super-conscious, or God or whatever name you want to give the all-knowing, ever-existing, ever-conscious creator. For everything and everyone is connected.

"The galaxies of light are the conscious world, and the particles of dark are the unconscious world. That is why we must go through the light of the spiritual eye to become fully awake to all that is and ever will be, my son. Then you will know the mind of God." She had an all-knowing, compassionate smile.

As Shakti was explaining the answer to my question, I could feel my entire body becoming hot. This intense heat seemed to rise from the bottom of my feet to the top of my head. And as this was happening, I could see my own aura appear around my body in bands of white, purple, and gold closest to my body. Then, as the bands expanded out further from my body, they became denser in shades of orange, green, and blue. It was amazing to me that I was able to understand all that she had been saying about how everything was connected and that by the use of deep meditation we could absolutely know the super-conscious mind.

It all became suddenly and completely clear, and I felt a tremendous sense of unconditional love spilling out from every pore in my body. I suddenly felt completely connected to all things. I felt that there was no separation between me and anything else. I knew without a doubt in my mind that I was one with the universe. Then, as I glanced down at my journal, I saw that even though I hadn't written down what Shakti had been saying—because I had been so overwhelmed by this feeling of oneness—the answers were all there in my own hand writing.

Then I remembered how Estrella had told me on the first day after my accident that thoughts were very powerful things and that everything comes into fruition after first being created by thoughts.

This is what Shakti must have done for me in my journal. She made sure I had everything that she had explained, written word for word, for me to refer to whenever I chose to.

Then, as I closed my journal, I again remembered being pulled through that dark tunnel after my accident and how wonderful it felt to be rushed through time and space and to see all the stars and planets and how they were being made from countless suns exploding and cooling. I also remembered during that experience how strange I felt, understanding that I was a part of all this great creation. And now, thanks to Shakti's answer, I knew for a fact that I had always been a part of everything, even though my tiny brain couldn't comprehend all of this while I was still alive in the human body.

I also came to know that if one thing were out of place in this great cosmic world, then everything would cease to exist. I don't know how I knew it, but of this fact, I was certain.

After Shakti finished the answer to my question, I began to realize that this feeling of wholeness and oneness with all creation was now slowly diminishing as I came down from this unbelievable experience.

Once again, I was aware of myself sitting in this large white room with everyone else, having our questions answered by these great, all-knowing beings.

Lord Aster then stepped forward and announced that we were all to become spirit guides. He told us not to get too excited yet, because we all still had much to learn before we would have our first assignments.

He then told us that we were to be paired off with a person of our choosing so we could help each other in our spiritual endeavors to become spirit guides. He also told us that if we already had someone in mind to partner up with, then we could do that now. Otherwise, Doshi Tow would assign someone to us.

Before I had a chance to consider whom I would pick for my partner, Sheila had placed her hand in mine and said, "I think we should be partners, don't you?"

A lump formed in my throat, and I had to swallow hard before I could answer her. I smiled and gently squeezed her hand and said, "You know, your right. I don't think we should break our link to each other. After all, it seems like we've always known each other, and it would be a shame if we lost each other now, don't you think?"

Sheila smiled shyly and nodded her head in agreement.

I wondered if I had known her in a past life, since I had such a strong connection to her. I didn't know if I'd ever have an answer to that question. But what I did know was that the connection I felt for her now was real and very strong, and I wasn't about to lose it.

Chapter 16

The Lists

Doshi ended our meeting by telling everyone that our question-and-answer session was over. He added, as if it were an afterthought, that in the future, if anyone ever had a question and needed an answer to it immediately and the guides weren't around to lend their assistance, all we had to do was open our journals, and we would find the answer already written there.

From the astonished looks on everyone's faces, I knew they were wondering just as I was how that could possibly be, but before anyone had a chance to ask him that question, he went on to says that the guides already knew what our questions were going to be, even before we knew them ourselves, and they had already written them in our journals.

As I thumbed through the pages of my journal the only things I saw were the answers to the questions that had been asked during our question-and-answer session and nothing more. I raised my hand to ask Doshi why I didn't have more in my journal, if the guides had already written the answers to our future questions.

And again, before I released the words from my mouth, Doshi said, "As you look through your books, you will notice that there is nothing more than what you have written yourselves from the questions you have already asked the guides. This is because when they write in your journals, the answers will not appear to you until you need them, even though they are already there."

Everyone seemed satisfied with that answer, since by now we were all becoming used to strange things happening around here.

Cory had partnered up with a young man named Elliott Thornton, who was rather short and stocky and reminded me of my best friend, Jake.

Elliott's hair, however, was jet black and very kinky, but neatly trimmed. His complexion was a light brown, but his eyes were dark brown, like mine. He seemed to be a very jovial young man, and even though I had just met Cory, they seemed to be a good match.

The two of them had caught up with Sheila and me as we commenced our long walk down the endless corridor to find the lists we were told about earlier.

After the introduction of our new friend, Elliott, we decided we would try to stay together as a team, if we had the good fortune to be placed in the same class together. So we interlocked our arms and said, "All for one and one for all." Then we slowly walked this long hallway with the hundreds and hundreds of other kids that had been at the meeting with us.

Finally, after what seemed like forever, we came to the end of the corridor and saw, taped to the wall, many sheets of paper in several rows. These pieces of paper were filled with the names of all the students that had attended the meeting we had just come from and indicated where each student would go and who his or her guide would be.

The lists were sectioned off in groups, with large letters of the alphabet strategically placed above each grouping. There was also a big sign hung above each row of names; which simply stated in bold red letters, Search for Your Name in Alphabetical Order, Last Name First.

So at this point, we had to split up to find our names in our particular grouping, but we promised to meet back up again in the great white chamber where we had our first meeting just as soon as we found out who our new teachers would be.

I found the line for my name under the grouping signified by a large letter *P*. Luckily I wouldn't have to wait too long before I reached the several lists beginning with that letter, since it was not a very common initial for last names.

Finally I was up to the wall, and I found my name on the very last list under the grouping *P* for last names. As I ran my finger across the page adjacent to my name, I found that my classroom number was 762 and that I was still going to have Doshi as my guide. But next to his name, in fine print, it stated that from time to time there would be another guide to take his place when he was unavailable.

When I opened my journal to write this information down so I wouldn't forget, I found on the first page that this information had suddenly appeared before I had a chance to put pen to paper.

"Wow, this is so cool," I said out loud without thinking. I closed my book and headed back down the long stretch of hallway to wait for my new friends.

***

Cory and Elliott found their names at about the same time and managed to meet each other in the corridor as they were walking back to the meeting room.

"Cory," Elliott said. "Who's your teacher and what room are you in?"

Cory said, "That little Asian guy named Doshi Tow is my new guide. How about you? Who is your guide and what room are you in?"

"My room number is 762, and I have the same guide as you," Elliott happily replied.

"That's great," said Cory. "I also have room 762. Now all we have to do is keep our fingers crossed that Lancer and Sheila also have the same guide and room number."

***

Once Elliott and Cory reached the great meeting room again, I saw them and waved to them, motioning them to come over to where I had three empty chairs waiting. We were all overjoyed when we found out that we all had the same guide and could stay together like we'd hoped. But we were still waiting for Sheila to get there and were wondering what was taking her so long.

"Maybe I should go and see if I can find her," I said. "I'm beginning to get a little worried. Maybe she didn't remember where we said we would all meet up." I was a little worried, but more than that, I secretly wanted to have a little alone time with Sheila before we met back with the guys.

Cory said, "We'll hold the fort down here until you two get back." Then he playfully slapped me on the back and gave me a wink, as if to say he understood how I felt about Sheila.

As I was walking back down that endless hallway, there was still a steady stream of kids who had not yet made it to the lists to find out who their guides were going to be. My eyes were darting back and forth from one side of the hall to the other to make sure I didn't miss Sheila in this massive throng of people. Then at last I saw her. Her tiny form was pressed up against the wall as she inched her way through the large group of kids going in the opposite direction.

"Sheila," I called out. I waved my hand back and forth to get her attention.

She was holding her journal tight against her chest to ensure she wouldn't lose it, and she continued to move ever so slowly back down the hallway. She appeared not to have heard me the first time I called to her. So again I called out her name. "Sheila, over here," I said, cupping my hands like a megaphone up to my mouth.

She finally looked up and saw me trying to make my way to her through the throngs of kids still moving in the opposite direction.

When I finally managed to maneuver to the other side, where Sheila was standing, she smiled and gave a big sigh of relief that showed me she was glad she didn't have to walk back all alone through this crowd of strangers.

"I'm so glad I found you," I said as I took her hand in mine to give her a sense of security.

"I am too. I wasn't sure if I would be able to find you and Cory and Elliott among all these people."

We kept as close to the wall as we could, making our way back to the great meeting hall. This wasn't exactly the kind of alone time I was hoping for, but it was still good to have her all to myself in this endless sea of people.

"Do I dare hope that we have the same guide?" Sheila asked?

"I still have Doshi Tow, who is the one who brought me here from my last excursion at the cemetery where I was buried. I mean, where my physical body was buried. And my classroom number is 762, just like Cory and Elliott."

"Oh, how wonderful!" Sheila exclaimed with delight. "I have the same guide as all of you and the same class. Now we can be the team that we wanted to be."

After meeting back up with Cory and Elliott, we set off to find room 762. There were several guides dressed in yellow robes mingling around the chamber and giving directions to students who were inquiring about the locations of their classes.

"May I help you, my children?" said a tall, lean guide with long brown hair and a long brown mustache to match.

I turned around and said, "Thank you, kind sir. We're looking for room 762, Mr. Doshi Tow's class. Can you help us?"

"Certainly, young masters," he said, pointing to the far side of the room.

As we all strained to see clear across this vast chamber, we could make out the number 762 on the wall, and directly beneath the number was the outline of a door, which was barely visible because it was the same color as the wall and blended in almost completely.

"Thank you so much," Sheila said to the man who pointed us in the right direction. The rest of us echoed her words of gratitude and we all hurried off in the direction that was pointed out to us.

Once we reached the other side of the room, we noticed an inscription on the wall: To Room 762. There was an arrow pointing down to the door. There was no doorknob or handle, so Cory just pushed on the door, and it opened.

After stepping through the door, we realized that it didn't lead to a room at all, because we were outside. This was the same patio that Doshi had brought me to when we first arrived. It had the same big white planters on each corner of the shiny white patio, separated by heavy white stone benches.

"What do we do now?" Elliott asked as he tried to push the door opened from the outside with no luck.

"Hmm," I said. "We were told that if we had a question, all we had to do was look in our journals and we would find the answer."

When I opened my journal, I saw written in my own penmanship, the following words, which I read aloud. "Follow the footprints that are emerald green." Footprints? What footprints? I looked around. I didn't see any footprints. Exasperated and worried that we had stepped through the wrong door, I closed my journal, and instantly, many sets of different colored footprints appeared, all leading away from the shiny white patio into a lush Garden of Eden.

"Hey," Cory said as he remembered our pens turning colors when we had a question for the guides. "These foot prints are the colors of each of the guides. Remember our pens turning colors?"

"Yeah," I said. "Emerald green is the color for Doshi Tow. I pointed to a set of emerald green footprints crisscrossing the other colored prints.

So off we went again, arm and arm, chanting, "One for all and all for one." And we followed the emerald-green footprints through a beautiful, lush landscape to find room 762.

After walking some distance, the beautiful landscape of rolling hills and lush plants came to a screeching halt. It looked as if the world we were on had just dropped off into nothingness, but the emerald-green footprints continued out into a black abyss, without so much as a star to light the enormous black sky. The only lights that could be seen were the effervescent emerald-green footprints, which glowed through the black space, appearing to be suspended in midair or just floating on nothing—nothing at all.

Clutching my arm tight, Sheila asked, with a not-so-subtle tone of fear in her voice, "What do we do now?"

I put my hand on hers in a reassuring gesture and said, "When all else fails, turn to your journal." I gave a half-hearted laugh.

Sheila opened her journal, and it read, Keep Going. You're Almost There.

"I don't know about the rest of you, or what kind of experiences you had when you crossed over," I said. "But for me, I remember flying through space and time, and I know it's possible to walk out into this nothingness and still be all right. After all, what could happen to us? We are already dead, at least to the physical body, aren't we?" I moved one step closer to the first step out into nothingness.

"Yeah, you're right," said Cory. "You go first, my man." He gave me a slight shove, which moved me even closer to the edge.

Even though I instinctively knew we would be all right, I said, "Okay, Sheila, you put your hands around my waist." Not only did I want to feel the closeness, but I wanted to make sure she hung on securely as we walked on these seemingly floating footsteps. "And, Cory, you put your hand on Sheila's shoulder. Elliott, you can bring up the rear by putting one of your hands on Cory's shoulder, and we will all go together. Me first, of course." I tried to show that I was brave.

I slowly put one foot, then the other, out into the nothingness, taking care to place my feet right on top of the emerald green footprints. And I was followed by the rest of our little group.

Chapter 17

Lesson One: Meditation

Finally our little group came to the end of the emerald green footprints, which led directly to room 762. The nothingness that we had trod for the last several minutes had once again ascended to a land that was full and lush, with every kind of tropical plant known to man.

It was good to be on solid ground again, and the sweet scent of honeysuckle filled our souls with a renewed vigor as we stood beneath a large flowering arch that beautifully framed a massive wooden door. The door was intricately carved with the symbol of *Om*, signifying the sacred syllable of the divine consciousness. And below that was the number 762 stenciled in an iridescent emerald green. Next to the number was Doshi Tow's name, carved in a lovely script, and I couldn't help thinking how beautiful it was and that it gave his name the honor it deserved.

A large golden doorknob was prominently placed at the center right of the door. And an emerald green welcome mat lay on the doorstep to invite students to come in.

"Well, are you just going to stand there or are you going to open the door?" Elliott said, with a little impatience in his voice.

"Okay, I said, with the same irritation in my voice. Then I realized that I shouldn't have been so sharp with him. Something within me prompted me to keep myself calm and even minded. I knew that I should not let others disturb my peace. So with a much calmer tone I said to him, "I was just admiring this beautiful door."

The knob was smooth and cool to the touch as I turned it and pushed open the door. It opened to a large but welcoming room with no chairs or desks. In place of chairs, there were many plush cushions, in a variety of sizes and colors, placed symmetrically in neat rows facing the front of the room.

At the front of the room was an altar on a long, narrow, elegantly draped table. The altar had been precisely arranged with photos of great saints and sages, many of whom I knew, but there were a few that I did not.

Each photo was adorned with beautiful flower lays, draped meticulously and reverently across the top of the ornate gold frames that housed the images of these people. The lays hung in such a way that the flowers made a beautiful, delicate necklace, which framed the faces of each divine being. Candles of all sizes glowed softly at their wicks, illuminating the altar and the divine faces of all the masters positioned there. I also noticed an incense stick burning in a small brass container at each end of the table, creating a stream of swirling smoke, and the smell of sandalwood wafted through the room.

Gorgeous mauve and gold silk drapes hung elegantly against large stained-glass windows on each side of the room. The floor was covered with a plush, off-white pile carpet that contrasted with the many multicolored cushions on the floor in rows of ten. The walls had been painted the color of a sandy beach, and all kinds of symbols of astrological signs were stenciled across the top edge as a boarder in a glowing yellow glitter.

"Come on," Sheila said. "It looks like we are the first one's here again, so we have our choice where we want to sit." She hurried to a bright pink, very plush cushion on the front row, right in front of the altar. Not wanting to be separated from her, I sat on a green, not-so-plush cushion right next to her. Cory and Elliott plopped themselves down on the next two cushions to my right, one red and one blue, and began chatting between themselves in low whispers.

"I wonder what our first class will be like," Elliott said as he leaned over to Cory and nudged him with his elbow.

"I don't know, but it looks like some kind of religious class," Cory said as he looked around the room.

It wasn't long before Doshi Tow entered the room and sat on a semi-flat green cushion that had been placed on a slightly raised platform at the front of the classroom, just left of the alter. As we watched Doshi from our front row cushions, he smiled at us and then placed a finger to his lips, as if to say, "Quiet, please. No talking."

Soon we could hear the door behind us opening and closing several times and people shuffling around to find the cushions that best suited them. Several times I looked at Doshi. He smiled at those who were entering and again brought his finger to his lips to let them know that silence should be observed at this time. The once-low murmur of the other students chatting excitedly soon stopped in response to Doshi's visual instruction.

After several more minutes, the door opened and closed for the last time, and Doshi again looked around the room and smiled at everyone present. "My dear children," he said as he continued to sit in the lotus position upon his green cushion. "I am Doshi Tow, a bhakti yogi, and I am so very happy to have you all in my class. It is my great pleasure to be instructing you in the art of being a spirit guide."

I didn't know that being a spirit guide was an art, but maybe it was. So I continued listening intently, making sure I didn't miss a single word he was saying.

"The first and most important part about learning the art of being a spirit guide is to know yourself completely. If you don't know who you are inside and out, how will it be possible to help others of your kind? My dear children, I want you all to feel absolutely comfortable in my relationship with you. Please don't feel afraid to ask me anything that you need or want to know. I am here for you so you can be there for others."

A student near the middle of our group raised her hand to ask a question.

"Yes, my dear Dorothy," Doshi said. "What is your question?"

"You said at our other meeting that this would be a get-acquainted secession. So could you please tell us something about yourself that would make us feel more comfortable with you? It seems you already know everything about us. I mean you already know who we are without us even telling you who we are. I feel the least you could do is tell us something about yourself." She lowered her head, almost ashamed to have asked such a question.

Doshi smiled and stood up to answer her. "Yes, my dear Dorothy and all of you, it is true that I know each and every one of you thoroughly. And that is why I have chosen each and every one of you to be in my class. I know you are ready for this high honor to be trained as spirit guides. Now, as Dorothy has stated, it's only right that you know something about me, so here it is. I was born on earth in the year 1120 in a little Korean village of about eighty-five people. I had two brothers and three sisters. This was my first incarnation on earth, and since then I have been reborn many times to this earth plane. I wasn't always of Asian descent, just as each of you weren't always of the race that you know yourselves to be now."

There were many surprised sounds in the classroom, because several of the students didn't know they had been reincarnated before. But I remembered Estrella telling me this when I first met her, when I awoke to find myself in the plain white chamber after my accident.

Doshi continued his explanation of his life's experiences. "I have been blessed greatly in my last few lifetimes to have been in the presence of more than one great one who knew their oneness with the universe, and it was through them that I was taught the art of meditation. Through the great method of meditation, I came to know who I really was and therefore am able to teach others this same procedure so they too can learn of their true nature. I have had good times in my many lives and bad times too. I have had heartaches and great joys. I have felt tremendous anger and great hate and wonderful happiness and unconditional love. There isn't an emotion that I have not experienced and known, so there is nothing that any of you should be ashamed to confide in me or ask of me."

Elliott then raised his hand.

"Yes, Elliott, go ahead and ask your question," said Doshi.

"Can you please tell us again exactly what a Bhakti Yogi is?"

"With pleasure, my son. A Bhakti Yogi is a person who reaches union with God, or super-consciousness, through the spiritual approach of all surrendering unconditional love as the principal means. There are other means to achieve this goal, such as Karma Yoga (union through work or action) or Jnana Yoga (union through wisdom and reasoning), just to name a few. But I, young master, have chosen the bhakti method because I have such a great devotion and love for the greatest creator of all times."

Cory, anxious to get his question answered next, waved his hand impatiently back and forth to make sure Doshi saw him; although, I don't know how he could have missed him, since we were on the front row.

"Go ahead, young Cory," Doshi said with a half-smile, half-frown on his face, trying to look displeased with him. But we all knew he wasn't.

"What should we call you? Should we call you sir, lord, Doshi Tow, Mr. Tow, or what?" He hoped his question wasn't too silly, but he wasn't quite sure how he should address him.

"No of course not Cory, my son, your question isn't silly at all. You may call me Doshi, as we, or all of us I must say, are friends and brothers and sisters in the great divine consciousness, and as such, we should all feel free to call each other by our first names. Don't you think so, young master?" There was a twinkle in his eye.

"But, Doshi, why do you keep calling me and others here young masters?" Cory said before Doshi had a chance to call on someone else. And he wondered how he thought his question might be silly, when he had only thought those words and didn't voice them out loud.

"Because you are all on a path to becoming masters in your own right," Doshi replied. "Someday everyone in this room will have attained the full realization of their oneness with the creator of all, the super-conscious supreme being, the father and mother of all the universes and everything within those universes."

As I looked around the room I saw that everyone was wide-eyed and awestruck by what they were hearing from our instructor. Yet, for some strange reason, I wasn't at all surprised at what Doshi was telling us. And I was fascinated with the intuitive way that I knew for a fact that everything Doshi was saying was the absolute truth. I wasn't sure how I knew it, unless this knowing came to me during the time when Shakti was giving me the answer to my question at our last meeting and I had that wonderful experience of feeling so completely whole and one with everything. It must have been something in that experience that gave me the ability to intuitively know if something was true or not. I marveled at this newfound ability and hoped that I would never lose it.

Sheila raised her delicate hand to pose her question to Doshi.

"Yes, child," Doshi said as he pointed to Sheila.

"If you please, dear Doshi, I would like to know what our first lesson will be about and what our class schedule will be."

"Our first lesson, my dear one, will be on meditation. I will teach you all how to meditate so you can understand your true nature and your relationship with all that is. I was going to start your first class tomorrow morning at five, but I decided that since you are all here now, this would be a good time to have your first lesson." Doshi Tow had a broad smile on his face. "Thereafter, each class will start at five o'clock sharp, and I expect everyone to be on time. Are you all in favor of starting your first lesson now?"

The entire class simultaneously responded in the affirmative with loud applause that lasted for a good long while. Then Doshi rang a small gong and motioned for everyone to quiet down.

"My dear students," Doshi said. "This instrument simulates the sacred sound of *Om*, also pronounced Aum, it is the Sanskrit word symbolizing that aspect of the Godhead that creates and sustains all that is. It is an actual cosmic vibration, and without this vibration there could be no physical or material substance. You may be surprised to know that even thought is a vibration, and it is this thought vibration or syllable that brings everything as we know it into manifestation.

"We will start our meditation by first taking three very deep breaths. You will breathe in very deep from the bottom of your diaphragm, expanding your abdomen and holding that breath for five seconds. Then you will exhale that breath to a count of five. You will then repeat those steps two more times, until you have made your three deep inhalations and exhalations. Once your breathing exercise is complete, I will ring the gong one time so you can experience the sacred vibration of the tone. When the note has finished its vibration, we will all chant the sacred syllable of *Om* three times, then rest our minds in the space of no thought.

"Okay, let's get started. Today, our meditation session will last for about fifteen minutes. It will get progressively longer as we get accustom to quieting our minds."

After we were instructed in how our posture should be and how to place our legs on the pillow in the lotus position, we all did our breathing exercises and chanted the sacred syllable of *Om*. Then the room went silent.

All that could be heard was the quiet, soft breathing of the students, and I couldn't help wondering what was going on in their minds. Were they able to erase all of their thoughts like we were instructed to do? If so, I wondered why I couldn't empty my mind.

I tried really hard to block my thoughts, but as hard as I tried I couldn't still my mind for the life of me. Every time I tried to push those pesky thoughts out of my head, new ones entered to take the place of the old ones. My body began to ach from sitting in such an awkward position, and I could feel every twitch and itch that threatened to consume my mind.

Still I fought to make my mind blank, but the small, flattened cushion I was sitting on seemed to get flatter by the minute, and the plush carpet beneath it lost all of its comfort as well. It seemed that something within me was working very hard to keep me from succeeding in my endeavor to quiet my mind and meditate. Minutes seemed like hours, and I kept telling myself that soon, Doshi would tell us that our meditation session was over, but the discomfort of this tiny cushion on the hard floor was making the time move ever so slowly.

I look up and saw Doshi meditating on his cushion. He looked so serene, so blissful. His eyelids were slightly parted, and his gaze focused on the heavens. He had a peaceful half smile on his lips, and I wondered how he managed to sit so still. As I continued to watch him, I noticed that there wasn't even a sign of him breathing. None of the discomforts that were plaguing me seemed to bother him in the least. I wondered how he could sit there like that.

My legs were cramping now, and I longed to straighten them out in front of me. I looked around for a clock, but there were none anywhere in the room. Again I closed my eyes and tried to quiet my mind, but no sooner had I done that than Doshi announced that our meditation session was over for today. "What a relief," I thought as I straightened my legs out in front of me to stretch the tight muscles in my calves.

Cory and Elliott also looked like they had been in pain as they managed to stand and stretch one leg and then the other, as if they were getting ready for a fifty-yard dash.

Sheila, on the other hand, sprung right up with no problem at all and held out her hand to me, offering to help me up.

"How did you like our first class?" she asked me as she grabbed my hand in hers and helped me to stand.

I felt a little embarrassed at having to be helped up, but I liked holding her hand, so I gladly let her help me, although I tried not to look like I needed her help.

"I really enjoyed the breathing and chanting," I said. "But the meditating didn't go so well for me today. How about you, Sheila? Were you able to meditate okay?"

"Not really," she said. "There were short periods when my mind seemed to quiet down for a bit, and during those times I felt calm and at peace, but soon I found myself thinking about what my dorm would be like and what it would be like to actually be a spirit guide for someone. But I did think it went pretty fast for our first class didn't you?"

"No! Not at all. I could feel every muscle in my body screaming at me for keeping it so cramped up on that little cushion, and I couldn't wait until Doshi said our class was over. I know I shouldn't have felt that way, but I couldn't help it. I just hope he doesn't hold that against me."

I felt ashamed that I had done so poorly for my first lesson. There wasn't one single moment during the entire meditation that I felt calm and at peace like Sheila did. Why was this so difficult for me?

"Don't worry, Lancer," Sheila said. "I'm sure we will all get better the more we practice. I've heard that it took people like Doshi and the other masters many years to become proficient in the art of meditation."

That wasn't very comforting to me, but I just shrugged and said, "Yeah, I guess you're right."

Everyone was now chatting and stretching their sore muscles when Doshi said, "Students, may I have your attention please. Directions to your dorms are written on the front inside covers of your journals. You may all be dismissed now to get settled in and explore your environment. I will see you all back here tomorrow morning at five o'clock sharp. Until then, may you all enjoy the rest of the day, and be sure to get to bed early, because five o'clock comes pretty early if you're not used to getting up at that time."

Then Doshi blew out the candles on the altar and left the room.

Chapter 18

Exploring Our Environment

Following the directions in our journals, we quickly found our living quarters. The girls' dorm was a large pink adobe structure that sat on a small hill overlooking a beautiful tropical garden. The garden was planted with such precision that it almost looked like an old English garden, except that the plants were all tropical rather than just roses, tulips, and boxwood shrubs. And I must admit that the smell was quite heavenly indeed!

Two large palm trees framed the stained-glass entryway that led to the girls' living quarters. And two wrought iron benches that had been painted white were placed on either side of the sidewalk leading up to the entrance.

On the way to the girls' dorm, we had passed a rather large fountain, with two angel statues in the shape of children playing in the water. The fountain was surrounded with several benches for people to sit on and enjoy the magnificent water display as it sprayed out jets of water in many different colors. They also could take in the beauty of the little park that surrounded the fountain.

"Let's meet back at the fountain at six o'clock sharp," Sheila said as she disappeared through the beautiful stained-glass doors."

We had decided to explore our campus all together after we had left Doshi's classroom. We all agreed with Sheila and headed for the boys' dorm, which was about three hundred yards east of the girls' dorm.

The path to our dorm was very hilly and had many twist and turns in it, but it was beautiful, nonetheless. The large tropical plants and trees that lined both sides of the path made it seem like we were venturing into some unknown jungle, because not only was the foliage very lush and thick but the wildlife here was also plentiful.

There were tropical birds of every kind and monkeys that swung from tree to tree as they played with their young. I was just glad that these creatures were of normal size and not the giants that I had seen when I was with Lord Aster. I recalled all to clearly the time I was in Jake's backyard and was only the size of an ant.

We finally arrived at our dorm, which was as large as the girls' dorm, only it was made of beautiful gray stones, which reminded me of the ancient medieval castles that I had seen in one of my history books.

The great, wide, ornate wooden doors leading into the building were flanked by two very massive blue spruce trees that must have stood some seventy-five feet tall, and at their base they must have been twenty-five feet around.

On the massive doors were two brass door handles. The doors opened in an outward direction. There was also a small peephole about three quarters of the way up on each door, so if you had a mind to, you could look out and see who was there before they opened the doors for them.

The stairs leading up to the massive doors were made of silver-streaked marble, and once on the landing there were two white stone benches set on either side of the door, facing each other.

"Man, can you believe this place?" Cory said as we marched up the four wide steps to the landing in front of the massive door.

"It's like nothing I've ever seen before, except in one of my history books when I was in high school," I said as I gazed up at the huge building. "It looks like an ancient medieval castle." I pictured King Arthur and the Knights of the Round Table sitting in the king's court, planning the defense of the kingdom from some wicked wizard.

"I wonder how many people can be housed in here?" Elliott mused out loud.

"I don't know, but I hope we don't get lost in here," I said as I opened the door and stepped into the foyer.

The floors were solid marble, and the walls were made of some kind of expensive-looking dark paneling. I wasn't sure what kind of wood it was, but the banisters on the stairs and the wood used for the chair rails were solid mahogany. I was sure of it because of their beautiful reddish-brown luster.

Everything was polished to a fine shine that really showed off the beautiful design of the wood grain, and I hesitated to touch anything, for fear of leaving smudgy fingerprints and ruining someone's hard work.

"Okay, now where?" Elliott said as he thumbed through his journal looking for directions.

"Elliott," I said. "At the front of our journals, it told you what your room number would be, don't you remember?"

"Yeah, yeah, Lancer, I remember," Elliott said as he turned again to the front of his journal and found the number 317. "Here it is. Room 317. Do we all have the same room?"

"No," I said. "My room is right next door. It's 316."

"So is mine," Cory said as he put his arm around my shoulder. "My room is 316 too, he reiterated with a slap on my back. "I guess we're roomies, bro, so let's go fine our room."

On the wall in the foyer were signs with room numbers and arrows pointing the direction for each grouping of rooms. Our rooms were on the third floor since they were in the three hundreds so up the stairs we went, and down a long yet wide hall with antique-looking sconces hanging on either side of the hallway every few feet. Even though the walls were made of that very dark paneling, the hall was surprisingly light and cheerful. There was also a delightfully refreshing breeze from the air conditioning units that gave us renewed energy as we continued looking for our rooms.

"Here we go, Cory," I said to him as I pointed to the number 316 hanging above the highly polished mahogany door.

"And here's my room, right across from yours," Elliott said as he opened his door and went in to look around.

I then opened our door, and Cory and I entered a modest but neat room with two single beds and one window. There were two gorgeous walnut desks, each with its own chair, and we each had our own dresser and small closet. There was also a small bathroom and shower that we would have to share, but it too was spotless. The room wasn't elaborate or anything, but it was more than adequate for our needs.

I was surprised to see my name embossed above one of the closets and on one of the dressers and Cory's name on the other. And since I didn't have any clothes except what I was wearing when I died, I was even more surprised, as was Cory, to see clothes in both our closets and dressers that were the exact sizes we wore.

I laid my journal in the top drawer of my desk and then closed the drawer again. "I'm going to shower and change," I told Cory. "And then you can have your turn before we meet up with Sheila again."

"Okay, Lancer. I'll just pop in on Elliott and see how he likes his room. I'll be back soon, so hurry up, will ya?" Cory jokingly demanded.

***

Sheila found her room and freshened up in a nice warm bubble bath before putting on a beautiful, blue chiffon dress that hung gracefully to her ankles. She'd found it in her closet. Now she headed out to wait for the guys.

As she walked back to the colorful fountain, she marveled at the beautiful scenery and wondered how there could be so many different species of plant life in this one area. The smells were so intoxicatingly wonderful that she thought she could be mesmerized into a state of infinite bliss if she were to stay here too long. She thought about her first meditation class and how this would be the perfect place to lose all thought and drift off into a profoundly deep meditation and become instantly evolved into a higher spirituality.

Finally Sheila arrived at the fountain and sat on one of the many benches that surrounded the large water feature to wait for her friends to arrive.

As she sat there quietly admiring the beautiful fountain, Doshi Tow walked up to her. "I thought you would like this place, dear Sheila. Do you like your room as well?"

Turning in surprise to see Doshi standing there, she said, "Why, yes, Doshi. My room is lovely, and so is this place. It's so nice of you to ask."

"You are right, dear Sheila. This would make a wonderful place to meditate," Doshi said, even though she had not mentioned those thoughts to him. "In fact, many people come here to do just that."

"How did you know I was thinking that, sir?"

"Oh, my darling child, you don't need to call me sir," he said. "And I know many things. That is why I am your teacher."

"Is it you I should thank for all the beautiful clothes in my closet?"

"No, that was Shakti, my little dear. She made sure that all the students here had everything they would need while attending our school. I will go now and let you enjoy the beauty of this place while you wait for your friends. They will be along soon." He left as mysteriously as he had come.

It wasn't long before Lancer came into view, followed by Cory and Elliott a couple of steps behind.

***

"Hi, Sheila," I said, waving to her as I hurried up the path to the angel fountain to sit next to her before the other guys beat me to the punch.

I was lightly out of breath when I reached her. "May I have this seat?" I asked, motioning to the spot next to her.

"Certainly you may," Sheila said with a shy but enticing smile.

I sat down right next to her and asked how she liked her new dorm room.

"My room is very nice. I have my own bed, dresser, and closet, and everything looks like new. The bed has lots of pillows with frilly pillowcases and a beautiful soft comforter that looks warm and inviting. And I couldn't believe that my closet and dresser were filled with lots of clothes just my size, and the desk had all the paper and pens I could possibly use. And do you like my new dress? I found this in my closet. What do you think?"

"Man, oh man," I said. "I have never heard you talk so much before—I mean all at once." Ashamed that I'd said that to her, I quickly added, "Oh, but I didn't mean anything by that. I'm glad you liked your room. It sounds a lot like mine, except for the frilly pillows. And that dress looks really good on you."

When Cory and Elliott finally met up with Sheila and me, we decided we'd better get going if we wanted to see all of our new environment before we had to call it a night.

"Let's go this way first," Cory said, pointing in the direction of a narrow cobblestone path flanked by a neat row of little yellow and pink flowers.

"Oh, how lovely they are," Sheila said as she bent down to pick one of the dainty flowers. Then she brought it to her nose to breathe in its beautiful fragrance.

"I don't know if you should be picking those flowers," Elliott said as he looked around to see if anyone was watching.

"Oh, Elliott, don't worry yourself so," Sheila said. "No one will miss one little flower."

"Look," Cory said excitedly as he pointed to the place where Sheila had just picked the flower. Miraculously, another flower had just appeared in the same place where her flower had been seconds ago.

Seeing this, Sheila happily bent down again and picked a few more flowers to make a small bouquet. And once again, a few seconds later, more flowers appeared where she had just finished picking her little bouquet.

"This is wonderful!" Sheila said. "Beauty is everywhere, and even when we take beauty away, it is renewed again instantly. What a wonderful existence we have now." She began trotting down the cobblestone path.

Almost tripping over Cory and Elliott, I said, "Come on, guys. It's getting late." And I ran to catch up with Sheila.

We came to a large stone archway covered with a thick layer of tangled vines, and as we passed through the arch, we entered a large courtyard with a lot of activity going on. To our left was a large choir singing the most beautiful tunes and being directed by a slender angelic woman with long golden hair. They all seemed so happy and full of life.

And to our right there was a small group of people meditating in the lotus position like we had been taught in our first class. But just a few yards away, we saw other people meditating too, only these people were floating in the air. They looked as if they didn't even realize that they were up there.

"I think they call that levitating," Sheila said in a low whisper, trying not to disturb anyone."

"Wow!" I said. "I wonder if we'll be able to do that someday, once we get good at meditating." I watched them for a few minutes in awe.

Once we got to the other side of the courtyard, we saw people practicing their mind control by moving small objects with their thoughts. This fascinated me as I watched how stern some of the people looked trying to focus their concentration on the objects that had been placed on a long table in front of them. Some of the people looked downright hilarious, while others looked almost frightening in the way they furrowed their eyebrows.

Once we got to the other side of the courtyard, we exited through another archway, and then we came upon a bubbly little creek, about eight feet wide. The two banks were connected by a little stone bridge, and large plants with big leaves hung over the water's edge, as if they were straining to taste of the clear cool water below.

This place looked so serene and picturesque that it reminded me of home, where the water lilies and cattails played in the bog next to Mom's garden.

The birds and fireflies reminded me of the bullfrogs, crickets, and butterflies that used to live around the water lilies on our property, and I found myself longing to be home again.

"Lancer," Cory said as he nudged me in the ribs. "Where are you? You look like you just saw a ghost or something."

"Oh, nowhere, Cory," I said as I realized I'd been day dreaming and I didn't want to share my thoughts with him at that moment.

"Let's see what's on the other side," Elliott said as he headed for the bridge.

One by one, we crossed the bridge, each looking down into the water as we did, trying to catch a glimpse of a fish or two as the water rushed by below us.

The sun was beginning to go down, but we just had to see what was on the other side of the big hill that we had just stumbled upon after leaving the creek. The evening air was beginning to produce a gentle breeze, which lifted our spirits and renewed our energy as we explored our new surroundings. Once we reached the top of the hill, we saw a large rectangular building with a flat roof in the valley far below. Between the valley and us was a very dense jungle that looked almost impossible to traverse. But as we searched the tree line, we could make out a narrow road leading into the jungle, and we reasoned that it must come out somewhere close to the building on the other side.

On the roof of the building, we could make out that there were some bright red words written in the ancient text of Sanskrit, but none of us knew what it said. The building seemed to stretch for miles from north to south, and we could see the sun beginning to set behind it.

"What do you think that is?" Elliott asked as we all looked on in amazement.

"I don't know," I said. "But I think we will have to check it out later because it's getting late, and it will be dark soon." I thought we should start back now or be caught in the dark and unable to find our way back to our dorms.

"You're right, Lancer," Sheila said as she grabbed my arm and turned us around. "I'm not sure I remember the way back in the daylight, let alone in the dark."

I didn't think she was really afraid of getting lost. I think she just wanted an excuse to hold my arm. Anyway, I wasn't going to disagree with her, so we started back down the hill with Cory and Elliott following close behind, chatting about how we must come back here and check out that building.

"And soon!" Elliott said, as if he was on some kind of quest that had to be completed by a certain time.

As we reentered the courtyard through the back archway, we saw that everyone who had been there earlier had gone. We also noticed how quiet it was. There were no chirping birds, no buzzing sounds of insects, no night noises of any kind at all.

"This is kinda eerie, don't you think?" Cory said.

"What's eerie Cory?" I said, trying not to seem concerned.

"That there isn't any sound except our own footsteps," Cory said. "Don't you think that's a bit odd?"

"You guys, there's nothing to be concerned about," Sheila said in a reassuring tone. "With all the strange things we've seen since we've been here, you mean to tell me that you're worried because there are no night noises?"

Embarrassed by her common sense, I was quick to say, "Yeah, Cory, Elliott, we've all seen some pretty strange things since we've been here. This may seem out of the ordinary for us, but it's probably completely ordinary for here, so come on. We better get back to the dorms and get some shut-eye."

After saying good night to Sheila and watching her enter her dorm building, we quickly headed for ours to get a good night's rest before our 5:00 a.m. class the next morning.

Chapter 19

My Out-Of-Body Experience

Exhausted from everything we had done that day, Cory and I jumped into bed to get some much needed rest. We left Elliott at his door and assumed he had done the same, as he had been yawning most of the way back from our late afternoon and evening exploration.

No sooner did Cory's head had hit the pillow than I could hear him quietly snoring away the day's activities, so I decided I had better do the same.

The room was cool—just right for sleeping, but for some reason, I just couldn't relax enough to drift off to sleep. I kept thinking of Sheila and wondered why she seemed so familiar to me. I also thought about our first meditation class with Doshi, and I became frustrated all over again because I hadn't been able to clear my mind like we were instructed to do.

I remembered seeing those other people in the courtyard meditating with such ease, and a tinge of jealousy rose up within me. I wished I could master that art like them. I also remembered seeing several people levitating several feet off the ground, and I thought, "Oh, I'll never be good enough to do that!"

I tossed and turned and told myself that I must sleep or I would be no good for tomorrow's class. But sleep just kept eluding me, as a barrage of thoughts kept racing through my mind.

"Lancer," said someone in a soft whisper next to my bed. I thought it was Cory, but when I looked over to his bed across the room, I saw that he was still in a deep sleep. Again I heard my name being called. "Lancer, my boy." Then I recognized Doshi's voice and looked to the foot of my bed, and there he stood with a slight smile on his face.

"What are you doing here, Doshi?" I said.

"I have come to reassure you, my son, and to tell you that you mustn't worry yourself so. You are a very special student of mine, and I want you to feel at ease and at peace." He moved from the foot of my bed to the side and patted me on the arm.

"How can I feel at ease when my mind fights me every step of the way," I said. "I tell it to be still and try to push my thought away, but it's as if they are laughing at me, knowing that I have no control over them."

"Have you forgotten everything, Lord Aster has told you about meditation?"

Thinking back, I tried to make myself remember what Lord Aster had told me about meditation, but his words just weren't coming to me. It seemed as if everything he had told me had found a black hole to crawl into to hide and was determined not to come out when I called it. "I can't remember, Doshi. Please remind me. I don't know why I'm forgetting everything," I cried out in anger and frustration.

Then I looked at Cory, afraid I may have awakened him, but he was still fast asleep. "How can Cory sleep through my conversation with you?" I asked in a much more quiet voice.

"Because I have made sure that he doesn't hear us," Doshi said in his normal voice. "My son, you have it within you to be a great spirit guide, and someday, you will be. But the first thing you need to do whenever you feel anxious or you just want to clear your mind for whatever reason—like getting some sleep for instance—you need to remember to breathe. Your breath is your very life, so you need to watch your breath as it goes in and as it goes out. And with each inhalation, think the words, 'I am calm. I am peace.' And with your exhalations think, 'Be gone, negativity and restlessness.' Slowly visualize your body relaxing, from your feet to the top of your head. For instance, mentally say, 'I feel my right foot relaxing.' Then, 'I feel my left foot relaxing.' Then, 'I feel my right calf relaxing.' Then, 'I feel my left calf relaxing.' Do this all the way up your body, and by the time you get to the top of your head, your entire body will be in a state of deep relaxation. It will be as if you're asleep, but you will be fully aware of everything around you. Remember this exercise, and you will do well in your meditations."

I thanked him for his advice, and he wished me a good night. Then I saw a flash of bright light, and when the light had dissipated, Doshi was gone.

The next morning, as I still lay in bed, I stretched long and yawned wide and forced myself to a wake up.

I glanced over at the clock on the night stand next to my bed, which was set to go off at 4:00 a.m. so Cory and I would have time to shower, dress, and get to class on time. The clock said it was 3:30 a.m. I could have closed my eyes and pretended to sleep for another half an hour, but I was now completely awake, and I felt surprisingly refreshed and really good for so early in the morning.

Thinking back on my conversation with Doshi the night before, I wondered if he had really been there at the foot of my bed or if I had just dreamed he was there. But as I got out of bed, I decided it didn't matter if it was a dream or not, because the advice he gave me seemed sound, and that was all that mattered, because after using his relaxation advice, I was now fully rested and ready to start a new day.

I got up, showered, dressed, and was ready to go by the time the alarm went off, nearly jolting Cory out of his bed.

"Wake up sleepy head," I said as I threw off his covers, exposing his blue flannel pajamas. "We've got a class to go to."

Cory stared at me with a glare of contempt in his eyes for a few seconds then buried his face in his pillow.

"Come on, Cory, it's time to get up," I said again as I poured a cup of hot coffee from the pot that had been provided to each room in the dorm.

Cory slowly drug one foot and then the other out of bed, until both feet were flat on the floor. He sat on the edge of the bed trying to wake himself up.

I handed him the cup of coffee and told him I would meet him outside after he showered and got dressed.

The early-morning air was cool and fresh as I excited the dorm and walked a short distance away from the building, where I found some picnic tables and benches. I sat backward on one of the benches with my elbows propped up on the edge of the table as I leaned back and looked up at the stars that were still in the early morning sky.

It was beautiful to behold. There were no clouds at all, and the stars looked like billions of tiny diamonds sparkling on black velvet. Everything seemed so perfect, and I vowed that today I was going to be able to clear my mind and experience what meditation was really supposed to be like.

It wasn't long before Elliott came bouncing down the stairs from the dorm landing. He saw me sitting at the table not far from the front of our building.

"Hey Lancer, where's Cory?" Elliott asked as he jogged up to my table.

"He was just getting up when I came out here," I said. "Why don't you go see if you can get him motivated, Elliott, so we're not late for our second meditation lesson. If he's not out here soon, I may just have to leave without him because we're supposed to meet up with Sheila and walk her to class."

"He sounds like the kid who is rooming with me. Tyson is his name, I think, and he was still in bed fast asleep when I left the room," Elliott said. "Okay, Lancer, I'll run back up and see if Cory is ready yet. You go ahead and meet up with Sheila, and we'll catch up with you guys in a little bit. Don't worry. I will make sure Cory isn't late. I promise!"

So I got up and headed for the girls' dorm to see if Sheila was ready while Elliott ran back up the steps to check on Cory's progress.

When I reached the girls' dorm, Sheila was sitting outside on one of the wrought iron benches in front of her building, chatting with two other girls from her dorm.

She didn't see me approach right away, so I had time to really look at her and see how beautiful she was sitting there in an elegant, blue and gold sari, illuminated by a large street lamp positioned a few feet behind her.

Her long, beautiful red hair hung loosely about her shoulders and had a slight delicate curl at the ends, which gave her hair a bounce when she tossed her head back and forth as she talked to her new girlfriends. Her slender arms were adorned with several gold and silver bracelets that had a slight jingle when she gestured with her hands, and on her ears hung long glittery earrings that showed off the vibrant shine of her bright auburn hair.

As I got closer, I could see the profile of her beautiful face, and my heart skipped a beat when I saw her long thick eyelashes flutter as she was trying to make her point to the other girls. Her lips had a touch of pink lip gloss on them, making them full, wet, and shiny. And I didn't know if my heart could take much more of this beautiful vision.

Sheila then turned her head in my direction at the sound of my approaching footsteps. "Oh, hi, Lancer," she said. "I'm glad you're here.

I would like you to meet my roommates." She pointed first to a tall thin girl with a pixie haircut who was also dressed in a sari, only hers was all one color—purple—and she also had dangly earrings and several bracelets on both arms.

This new girl's face was not beautiful but not ugly either. She wore no makeup, and I thought that if she had, it might have helped her appearance some. "This is Helen Shuster," Sheila said. "And she's been in Doshi's class before, but Doshi wasn't teaching meditation at that time. Helen said he was teaching the art of silent communication, which sounds pretty cool, if you ask me. I hope we get to learn that sometime." Sheila hardly missed a beat between words.

I graciously shook Helen's hand and told her I was very happy to meet her. Then Sheila introduced the other girl.

"And this is Elaine Wyatt. She's new like us. She only just arrived last night, so she didn't get to attend Doshi's first class yesterday, but she says she's anxious to see what it's like today."

Again, I graciously took Elaine's hand and welcomed her to our group and told them that Cory and Elliott would be along in a few minutes.

Elaine was a petite girl with shoulder-length, coal-black, shiny hair and a fair complexion. Her voice was soft and sweet. "It's so nice to meet you too," she said.

Just then Elliott and Cory came racing up to us, after what appeared to be a sprint from the boys' dorm to the girls' dorm. They stood half bent over, trying to catch their breath for a few minutes before they made their greetings.

"I don't know if that's such a good way to start off the day when our first class is meditation," I told them. "I mean, we are supposed to be calm and serene, and won't it be hard to be calm and serene after running a hard sprint like that?"

"Oh, it's okay, Lancer," Cory said. "I just needed something to wake me up. After all, I'm not used to such early hours, you know."

So after Cory and Elliott made their introductions to the new girls, we all headed off for room 762, under the flower archway, to have our second meditation class with Doshi Tow.

Once we got there, I looked for and found a very thick cushion in the middle of the room and plopped myself down on it to see if it would be comfortable enough for me to sit on for the next hour or so. I managed to bring one leg up and then the other in a crossed lotus position and still felt quite comfortable, so I decided this would be my cushion from now on. Sheila again sat on the cushion right next to me, and the others members of our group found cushions in other parts of the room that suited them best.

"Why didn't you want to sit in the front of the class again, Lancer?" Sheila asked, leaning over to me as I tried to sit straight with my eyes closed.

"No reason—except I wanted a more comfortable cushion this time." I opened one eye and looked down at her as she looked up at me.

She could tell that I was trying to keep my spine and head straight, and we both started giggling at what must have been a strange response on my part, not looking at her with both eyes and turning my head toward her when she spoke to me. But our amusement soon quieted when Doshi entered the room, and everyone's attention was focused to the front of the room.

"Good morning, my children," Doshi Tow said as he bowed low before us.

This was his way of greeting everyone, and we didn't think anything of it. We all responded with a good morning to Doshi in return.

"First I would like to go over our quick lesson that we had yesterday," he said. It really wasn't meant to be a real class yesterday. As you know, we were just supposed to get acquainted, but I decided it would be good to have a short meditation session anyway to see how many of you really understood the concept of meditation. Yesterday, I noticed that several of you, in fact most of you, had trouble clearing your minds and entering the center of your being. Isn't that so, class?"

Many in the room answered in the affirmative. Doshi went on to explain again the process of meditation. Then he said, "Once again, after we do our deep breathing exercises and chant the sacred syllable of *Om*, I will ring the gong, and we will feel the vibration of the sacred syllable until it has finished. We will then clear our minds of all thoughts, except for that one thought that brings your consciousness to that center point in your heart, which creates a sense of calm. This will help you enter into your own soul. Once you have reached a state of calmness and you focus your attention at the spiritual eye and also the at the heart chakra, you will find that your awareness will start to become sharpened and that many of your questions will find answers."

Once our deep breathing and chanting were over, Doshi rang the gong, and the sound of the sacred syllable *Om* reverberated throughout the classroom. The powerful note seemed to bounce off the walls from one side of the room to the next and then the sound finally became softer and softer until there was no sound at all.

As I sat their erect, back straight and chin up, and my hands placed palms up on each knee, I felt much more comfortable and relaxed than the day before. I felt the vibration of the sacred sound of *Om* surge through my body as if it were sending an electrifying charge of energy all through me. Once the sacred note had stopped its spiritual vibration, I focused my concentration on the spot between my eyebrows known as the spiritual eye. It was strange to me that now I was able to remember everything that Lord Aster had explained to me in Jake's backyard, when earlier those memories just wouldn't come no matter how hard I tried to summon them.

I also remembered Doshi telling me that I should watch my breath, not with my eyes but with my awareness, and that I should say to myself with every inhalation, "I am calm. I am peace." And on every exhalation, I should mentally say, "Be gone, negativity and restlessness." So with full attention, I followed these instructions to the letter, and it wasn't long before I found all my restlessness and unwanted thoughts leaving my body.

Strange as it was, it felt like all the negativity and restlessness was being drawn or sucked out of my body from the top of my head, leaving me with a feeling of weightlessness. Nevertheless, I kept my concentration at the spiritual eye and continued to mentally repeat what Doshi had told me the night before.

There was still some doubt as to whether Doshi had actually appeared in my room last night or if I had just dreamed him there. But because of the advice I got, dream or not, seemed sound, I decided it would be a good idea to follow this advice, in the hope that it would help my meditation today.

The next thing I realized was that all feeling had left my body. I thought this more than a bit strange, because yesterday I could feel every itch and twitch my body made. So I opened my eyes a little, just to check and see if my body was still there.

When I opened my eyes and looked down, I expected to see my arms and legs, but instead I was completely flabbergasted to see my entire body, from the top of my head all the way down, sitting in the lotus position on my meditation cushion, still meditating. My eyes were slightly opened and focused at the spot between my eyebrows. And I could barely make out the slightest breath being inhaled and exhaled as my abdomen gently moved in and out.

This was incredible. I had evidently left my body, and now I was watching myself meditate as I hovered several feet above my own body. As I looked around the room, I saw all the other students sitting on their cushions, quietly trying to meditate.

Some of them were squirming, as I had yesterday, trying to get comfortable. Some were sitting straight, with their eyes closed and meditating properly—at least as far as I could tell. And others looked like they were actually asleep as they sat there, slightly slumped and snoring quietly.

And then I looked at Doshi at the front of the room, and I was astonished to see him looking straight at me—not at the me sitting on the floor but the me floating above my other body. He smiled at me and then he motioned with his eyes for me to look back at my body. When I did, I didn't see just one of me, I saw five of me. There was the original me, sitting on the cushion that I had picked out when I'd first entered the room. Then there was another me sitting to the right of the first me. Then there was another me sitting to the left of the original me, and one in front and one in back of me. They were all sitting in the lotus posture, yet I could tell they were all able to act independently of the other me, because one of them looked up at me at the same time I was looking down at him, while yet another scratched his knee, and another turned his head and looked at all the other versions of me.

A sudden awareness then came over me that gave me the realization that I was not this human form at all, but the pure spirit which inhabited all those human forms I saw of me. I also realized that I was a part of every human form not just my own, because spirit is everywhere, in and through all things at all times.

The next thing I knew, I was again back in my original body, sitting quietly on my meditation cushion, and all of the other forms of me that were here just minutes ago were now gone. I now felt the coolness of the room and reasoned that the air conditioning must have come on sometime during our meditation, yet I wasn't the least bit disturbed by this unusually cool condition. Still I felt an unbelievable calmness and peace, even after having such an incredible experience just a short time ago.

Suddenly I saw an incredible bright light at the point in my forehead where the spiritual eye is located, and I heard these words in my mind, just as clearly and precisely as if someone was talking directly to my face. "You, my dear Lancer, have the power within you to create all the undreamed of possibilities that the mind can fathom, so create well, my son. Create well."

The next thing my senses picked up on was the powerful reverberation of Doshi Tow's gong signaling the end of our meditation class for the day.

Chapter 20

The Counselor's Meeting

After leaving our class, Sheila and I, and the rest of our now ever growing little group since Elaine and Helen joined us, headed for the great dining hall for a bit of breakfast, and I must admit that after my tremendous experience during our second meditation class, I was quite famished.

Sheila and the girls were chatting excitedly about what they had experienced during the class, while Cory and Elliott talked about finding out what was in that big rectangular building we had seen just before sunset the day before as we explored our surroundings.

However, my mind was still whirling and quite dumbfounded by what I had just experienced in my meditation, and as I listened to the girls talk about their experiences, excitement in their voices as they described what seemed to me not to be anything too extraordinary, I decided that I should keep my experience to myself, at least for now.

As the six of us entered the dining hall, we saw that it was nearly full to capacity with students from not only our class but all the other classes combined. Everyone was chatting happily as they ate, creating an almost humming sound of sorts, since you couldn't make out any one person's conversation.

This time, instead of just sitting and being served like before, there was a long line of people leading up to a buffet of steaming delectable foods being served by people wearing white aprons and hairnets. The long line enabled those who were already eating, time to finish and leave their tables as the kids in line filled their trays.

The dining hall was bustling with people coming and going, and laughing could sometimes be heard over the constant humming of everyone's voices. Even though it was crowded, everyone seemed to be enjoying themselves immensely.

Finally our little group managed to move up to the buffet after we joked about who's stomach was growling the loudest, and we found ourselves grabbing trays, silverware, and napkins and sliding them down a long metal shelf in front of a glass window separating us from the food.

There was bacon and eggs, every kind of egg imaginable—scrambled, poached, fried, over easy, or raw in a glass so you could drink it. There were pancakes, waffles, fruit, yogurt, Jell-O, French toast, biscuits and gravy, or anything you could possible desire for breakfast, cooked and ready to be served up to us just for the asking.

While the girls picked only light stuff, like yogurt and toast, Cory and Elliott and I filled our plates with biscuits and gravy, scrambled eggs, toast, bacon, and a side order of pancakes. We also made sure to grab up a large orange juice and a carton of milk, and we headed for the table that the girls had already chosen for us, since they got their food first.

"You weren't hungry, were you, Lancer?" Sheila said, looking at my tray completely full of three different plates and two drinks as I sat down next to her. The other girls giggled, pointing out that Elliott and Cory also were eating like this was the last meal they would ever have.

"As a matter of fact, I am starved," I said as I dug into my food, hoping I wouldn't have to say anything more, at least until breakfast was over, because I really didn't want to be asked about my meditation experience, and that seemed to be all the girls were interested in talking about all the way to the dining hall and as we waited in line for our food.

"Boy, these cakes are the best," Elliott said, and he cut into another piece of the pancake stack he was working on.

"Yeah, they are," Cory confirmed. Cory then asked, "Say, guys, what do you say we go back to that building we saw yesterday at the bottom of the hill? I think we need to see what it's all about," he said to us as he swung his arm around my neck. It must have been what he thought he needed to do to persuade me to go.

"What building?" Helen asked in a sudden tone of excitement as she looked up from her yogurt.

"Yeah, what building?" Elaine repeated, in an equally excited tone, as she thought this must be something very intriguing by the way Cory had mentioned it. They could see how much Cory was really trying to talk us all into going by the way he played like he was twisting my arm."

Sheila jumped in. "Oh, it's just a really big, plain white building we found last night when we were exploring our surroundings," she said without too much enthusiasm. "We just happened upon it after climbing this really big hill on the other side of the creek. And some of us wanted to check it out yesterday." She pointed to Cory and Elliott. "But it was already getting late in the evening, and if we had gone down to check it out then, we would have had to find our way back in the dark, and none of us wanted that," she said to her two new girlfriends.

"Oh, I think that would be wonderful!" Elaine said. "It would be like an adventure. I'm all in. How about the rest of you?" She nudged Helen in her ribs with her elbow.

"Okay, I'm in too," Helen said, not wanting to be a party pooper. "Are you coming too, Sheila?" Helen asked, putting her hands together as if she were begging her.

"Yeah, I guess so, if the rest of you are."

"One for all and all for one," Elliott said as he put out his hand across the table in a gesture like the Knights of the Round Table to seal our new quest."

Then, following his lead, we all clasped our hands together and repeated his words, "One for all and all for one."

Just then there was a voice that came over a loud intercom: "Lancer Puckett, will you please come to the counselor's room immediately. That's room 101." Then the message was repeated one more time, and the announcer added, "Thank you."

Looking kind of embarrassed, like I had just gotten in trouble or something, I said, "Sorry, guys. I'll have to check out that building later, but you go ahead without me. You can tell me if it's anything really interesting or not."

As I got up to leave, Elliott put out his fist to bump knuckles with mine and said, "Hey, dude. You tell us if there's anything on your end that's interesting or anything we should know about."

"Yeah, yeah. I will. See you guys when you get back. I'm sure that whatever they want me for, it will be long over by the time you guys get back from exploring that building." I walked away, still wondering why I was being summoned to the counselors room."

As I walked down the long corridor on the east side of the dining hall, I noticed on the wall to my right a line of arrows every few feet, illuminated in a vibrant golden yellow, pointing my way to room 101. I noticed the color of those arrows waist high on the wall, and I quickly remembered the footprints that illuminated an emerald green path that led us to Doshi Tow's classroom on the first day.

Thinking this had to have some significance, I racked my brain to remember all of the colors that we were told our pens would turn when we wanted to ask a question to a particular guide. "What did she say to us?" my mind asked as I tried to bring back the memories of our question-and-answer class. "Let me see," I said under my breath. "Pastel pink was Estrella, and I know emerald green is Doshi Tow's color. What is Lord Aster's color?" I furrowed my brow, trying to remember. "Come on, Lancer," I whispered quietly as I continued down the hall. "Oh, what is it? What is it?" Then the light came on as if by magic. His color was ocean blue, and Shakti's color was a vibrant golden yellow. "That's it!" I said with a sense of satisfaction for remembering correctly.

These arrows must have been leading me to Shakti's room, because Shakti's color was vibrant golden yellow, like the arrows. But then I began to question my own reasoning, because these arrows were leading me to a counselor's room, and Shakti certainly wasn't a mere counselor. She was one of the top spirit guides, if not the very top spirit guide out of all of them. So how could this be Shakti's room? I hurried down the hall, following those vibrant golden yellow arrows midway up the wall to my right.

Suddenly the arrows came to an abrupt stop, and I looked up at the room number above the door where the arrows had ended. "Well, I'm here," I said, with a heavy sigh as I knocked on the door, thinking I must have done something wrong to have been called to the counselor's office.

As soon as I knocked on the door, it opened. Behind it was a small, tidy room with two plush white wing backed chairs facing each other. On the right hand side of each the chairs was a small glass side table, which held a candle, a string of beads, and a small round gold container with the picture of some ancient god or goddess engraved on the lid.

I stepped into the room, and the door closed behind me, leaving me all alone in this little room. I walked over to one of the chairs and sat down, thinking that the counselor would be here soon to scold me for doing something I shouldn't have done or perhaps for not doing something I should have done.

As I sat there, I thought it strange that no one was here in the first place to greet me, and I began to wonder if I had entered the wrong room.

I got up and went to check the room number again, but the door had no doorknob on the inside, and it wouldn't push open, so the only thing left to do was sit back down and hope someone would soon come and find me.

I began to think I needed to do something to past the time, so I decided it would be a good idea if I took this opportunity to practice my meditation again. So I closed my eyes and did my deep breathing exercises. Once that was done, I started chanting the sacred syllable of *Om* over and over again. We were told to chant it three times in our meditation class before we cleared our minds of all thoughts. I then remembered Doshi telling us that after our minds were calm and our thoughts had been stilled, we should focus our concentration on the spiritual eye.

I brought my focus to the point between my eyebrows, but a strange thing happened. Even though I had completed my three chants of the sacred syllable of *Om*, something deep within me kept chanting it. I knew I wasn't actually saying the syllable out loud, but the sound kept reverberating in my mind over and over again. And it was just as loud as if I was actually saying it.

I marveled at how this powerful sound had its own volition to keep repeating itself over and over again without any help from my conscious mind. It was as if this sacred note had taken over my mind and my body, and I was held captive to its enchanting sound.

I began to feel it filling my body with a fluid flow of energy and light and warmth. As I gazed at my hand, I could see that it was also fluid energy, vibrating to its own frequency, and I could feel the aliveness of my skin. And I found it strange that I had never thought of my skin as being alive before.

I closed my eyes again and listened to the sound of *Om* as it continued its deep rhythmic vibration in my mind, and I let myself experience whatever it wanted to give me.

As soon as I surrendered to the sacred note, the entire room exploded in such a brilliance of white light that even though my eyes were closed, it was almost blinding. The explosion of light lasted only seconds, and when the room once again dimmed to its normal brightness, I heard the unmistakable voice of Shakti saying, "Very good, Lancer. I knew you had it in you to be the great soul I know you will become. You may now open your eyes, child, my precious child."

I slowly opened my eyes and saw the beautiful vision of Shakti sitting in the chair across from me.

"I've been watching you, Lancer," she said with a sweet tender smile. "Not only in this lifetime, but in all of your past lives as well. You are called to be a great spirit guide, my child, and that makes you very special, Lancer Puckett. Very special indeed."

"And even though you are not aware of all your abilities at this time, my child, you will still be extremely helpful to those in need as you gain insight into your spiritual powers and awaken to your true self."

Her words surprised me. I couldn't imagine why anyone would think I was so special. As far as I was concerned, I was just an ordinary teenage kid, just like all of my friends. I wondered what it was that made me so special, and if I was so special, did that mean that my friends are special too, just like me?

"You are much more than your peers, Lancer," Shakti said to me, reading my thoughts. "And it's time you learned how to use your God-given talents so you will be able to help all those who will need you when your time here is done."

"Okay, I understand that I am here to learn to be a spirit guide, Shakti. But please explain to me what all these strange experiences are that I've been having in my meditations?"

"The experiences you have been having are signs that your soul is awakening to its true nature, my son, and it won't be long before you will be ready to help others on their upward spiritual paths."

"It is important for you to understand that the people you will be helping will have no idea they are on their own spiritual paths, nor will they even know you are helping them. However, young Lancer, with your help, they will evolve to a higher level of understanding of their own spiritual nature, thus their lives will be less troublesome and less fraught with worry. You will be helping them to overcome some of the trials they are going through due to their karma and giving them some sense of security and joy as they journey through their own life's experiences."

Wow! How could I, a kid from the small town of Overton Mills, be able to help others as Shakti was describing? I continued listening intently to every word she was telling me, knowing instinctively that her instructions were somehow very important to my spiritual growth.

"You see, dear Lancer, everyone is on a spiritual path, even those who don't believe in a higher power or a creator. Those self-proclaimed atheists, who cringe at the very thought of God or a higher power, are on their own spiritual paths, and they don't even know it. And yes, even those who are filled with hate and evil and who wish only to do harm to others for the mere pleasure of it are on a spiritual path, and someday they will come to realize how wrong they were and strive to change their lives for the better. But I want you to know, my son, that whether it takes just one lifetime or as many as a million lifetimes, everyone will eventually come to know the creator of all that is." The warmth of her holy aura seemed to penetrate to my very core and fill me with the truth of what she was saying.

"Wow, that's reassuring," I said. "It's good to know that everyone, even the worst of the worst, will someday come to know the creator of all."

"Yes, that's right, my child. Now, you see those beads beside you, my son?" Shakti said, pointing to the small side table next to my chair. "Those beads have been blessed by me and are a gift to you to use while chanting your mantra. They are called Mala Beads, and there are 108 beads to each strand. The reason each Mala strand has 108 beads is because the chakras in each human body are the intersections of 108 energy lines, which converge together to form the Heart chakra. One of these energy lines, the Sushumana, leads to the Crown chakra, and is the path to self-realization. And the 108 beads represent these energy lines in the human body. These beads are used to count the number of times you chant your mantra, my dear Lancer. Positive mantras are always good and beneficial to the one using them, but I will give you a special mantra to use that will speed up your self-realization."

"What exactly is a mantra?" I asked, even though I vaguely remembered Lord Aster telling me about it when he was teaching me how to meditate in Jake's backyard. Lord Aster gave me examples of some mantras, but I didn't really know how to use them or what they would do if I did use them.

"A mantra is a sacred incantation the yogi uses to help bring his consciousness closer to the divine intelligence or the creator of all," Shakti said. "The mantra I will give you has a great power instilled within it to swiftly bring you to enlightenment, but you must keep it secret, my dear, because a mantra is very personal and designed only for the one to whom it has been given by a supreme being. You could even say it has been super charged with divine energy to awaken the supreme intelligence within you."

Glancing back to the side table, Shakti continued. "I'm sure you also noticed that little gold box on the table next to the mala beads. It contains a sacred ash called Vibhuti. The spiritual aspirant, to aid in his or her meditations, also uses this, because it is very powerful and helps to invoke the right energy into his or her subconscious mind. It helps to keep you focused. The way a spiritual aspirant uses this sacred ash is by dipping the ring finger of his or her right hand into the ash and then placing it at the point between the eyebrows known as the spiritual eye."

I already knew about the spiritual eye because I remembered Lord Aster explaining that to me when we were in Jake's yard. But I didn't know about this sacred ash or the mala beads. So I carefully listened as Shakti explained their use.

"I want you to take these and use them daily during your meditations. You need to meditate regularly, every morning before you get out of bed and every evening before retiring. Keep these things with you always. And remember, you don't need to limit your meditations to twice daily. You may meditate any time you feel the need or desire and for as long as you want, but never leave a meditation if you have not first felt the presence of the divine intelligence, which dwells deep within each of us. I am very proud of you Lancer. Stay true to your course and you will be on your way to helping others very soon."

I thanked her for her kind words, and for the mala beads and Vibhuti, and I told her that I would use them faithfully.

"Okay, my dear Lancer, you may go now. I'm sure you are anxious to meet your friends again. Oh, just one more thing, Lancer. What was said in our meeting today is to be kept confidential. Your friends are not quite ready for this information. But don't worry about them my son. Their time will come soon enough."

As she stood to indicate that our meeting was over, she placed a small piece of paper in my hand and said, "Lancer, here is your sacred mantra; you must memorize it and then destroy this piece of paper." Then she motioned me to the door with a graceful wave of her arm and smiled warmly.

I thanked her once again and bowed low, showing her the respect that she most certainly deserved as a supreme being, and I left through the now opened door.

Chapter 21

The White Building

"Come this way," Cory said as he motioned to the new girls, pointing them in the direction of the creek and then to the little bridge that connected the two banks. "We have to cross here and then take a little walk up a hill before we can see the white building."

"Yeah," said Elliott. "And then it's a short walk down the hill and into some big forest before we come out on the other side to the white building."

Sheila gave a heavy sigh, as if she really wasn't into this whole adventure thing. But not wanting to fall behind, she quickened her steps to catch up with Helen and Elaine, who for some strange reason Sheila couldn't understand, just couldn't wait to find out what that big white building was all about.

Elliott and Cory had made it sound so mysterious and intriguing by wondering out loud what was in it. They speculated that maybe it was a prison for all the people who died and had done evil deeds while on earth. Or maybe it was where all the enlightened beings lived. Or perhaps it was where students went when they graduate from spirit guide classes.

Elliott told Elaine and Helen that the building looked foreboding, because he hadn't seen any windows the first time they saw it during their grounds exploration. So it had to be a place of punishment to keep those inside from enjoying any fresh air and beauty. However, Cory thought it looked more like a place to store things, like food and supplies and stuff that everyone would need while they were here.

***

"I don't know why I'm not as curious as the rest of our group to find out what's in that building," Sheila thought as she begrudgingly walked just behind Elaine and Helen, with Cory in the lead and Elliott bringing up the rear.

She really had no interest in finding out what's in the building. She just came along for the ride, so to speak, so she didn't have to be in her dorm room alone. She'd rather have been with Lancer, her newfound friend and partner, but she knew counselor's meetings were private, meant only for the counselor and the students, but she wished she'd waited for him all the same.

Finally Sheila decided since she couldn't change the fact that she hadn't waited for Lancer and she was now halfway to the white building with her friends, that she would try to make the best of the little outing so she wouldn't be a drag for everyone else.

Finally they arrived at the base of the large hill they'd climbed the day before.

"Man, oh man, that's a large hill!" Elaine said. "How long did it take you guys to climb it?" She leaned against a tree to rest for a minute.

"Oh, come on, Elaine," Helen shouted back to her as she and Cory started trotting up the hill.

"Don't tell me your tired already," Elliott said as he grabbed her by the hands, pulling her away from the tree she was leaning against.

"Oh, no, I'm not tired, trying not to be a party pooper." "I was just taking in the view."

"You ain't seen nothin' yet," Elliott said. "Just wait until you get to the top. Then you will really have a view."

Sheila had caught up with Helen and Cory as they trotted up the hill, while Elliott pulled Elaine away from the tree she had been resting on. "I don't remember this hill being quit so big the last time we climbed it," she said to Cory as she huffed and puffed with every upward stride.

"Of course not. You were too busy holding Lancer's hand to notice anything else," Cory said with a little smirk on his face.

She pretended not to hear Cory's sarcastic words and hoped that she and Lancer hadn't looked too silly the day before, while they walked hand in hand. Sheila didn't want anyone to think she was being too clingy and get the wrong idea about her and Lancer. It was just that she felt so connected to him. She knew there was a very special bond between them. What it was, she just couldn't put her finger on, but when she was with him it felt so good and so natural, and she didn't want to ever loose that.

"I think we should stop and wait for Elaine and Elliott," Helen said as she looked back to see them trailing some fifteen to twenty yards behind.

"No, come on you guys," Sheila said. "We're almost to the top, and we can stop there if you want to, but let's not stop yet. It's just a few more yards."

This time, both Cory and Sheila grabbed hold of one of Helen's hands and pulled her forward, urging her to continue just a few more yards to the top of the hill.

Once they finally arrived at the precipice, they collapsed to the ground and surveyed their surroundings. The view was gorgeous! They were able to see for miles in every direction, and the colorful landscape was truly breathtaking.

The valley below lay just beyond a dense forest, which stretched as far as they could see to the north and to the south, but to the west, on the other side of the forest they could barely make out the outline of the large white building they'd seen the evening before. It was apparent that they were at least a couple of miles from the point that they had climbed yesterday, because at that time, they could see the building more clearly, and it seemed much closer.

"We must have miscalculated exactly how we came yesterday," Sheila said to Cory, who had been leading them.

"Yeah, you're right, but we still see the building. We'll just have to walk a little farther, that's all," said Cory.

"Well, what do you expect?" Elliott said. "It was beginning to get dark when we came yesterday, and things look different in the dark, you know?"

"Not really," said Sheila. "It was only dusk when we started back. That's why we decided to go back, so we wouldn't have to find our way back in the dark."

"All right, guys," Helen said. "Let's not argue about this. We're here, and I still want to know what's in that building."

Finally Elaine and Elliott arrived at the top, and both collapsed to their knees, exhausted and acting as if they had walked for days.

"What a beautiful view," Elaine said when she finally caught her breath and stretched out her legs to work the kinks out.

The sun was now straight overhead, but light clouds intermittently dotted the sky. There was a slight breeze that moved the clouds, bringing bits of welcome shade to their little party.

As they viewed the landscape, trying to determine what their next step would be, they saw a tiny trail, vaguely visible, leading into the forest below.

"Look over there," Helen said, pointing in the direction of the trail.

"Yeah, I see it," said Cory. "It's a trail leading into the forest. That must be the way through the forest. I'm sure it will lead us right out on the other side next to the building."

"Let's go," said Elliot. "We still have a ways to go, and the clock is ticking." He offered his hand to help Elaine to her feet. Cory then did the same for Helen and Sheila, and off they went down the hill.

Soon they found the trail that led straight into the forest, and one by one they went from a bright sunny warm day to almost pitch black, as they each entered under the thick canopy of the towering fir trees.

The air felt cool and damp, and a musty order fell heavy over their little party as they marched single file farther and farther into this foreboding jungle.

"Listen guys," said Elliott.

"What is it?" Helen nervously choked out.

"That's just it," Elliott said. "I don't hear anything. There is absolutely no sound at all. Shouldn't there be sounds of birds or insects or something."

"Oh, don't worry about it," Cory said. "I'm sure there's nothing in here that can do us harm. After all, we're already dead. I mean, you know, we're spirits now, so we can't die again."

"How do you know?" Helen said. "We've died many times before. Who's to say that we can't die again? Maybe we will be transformed into something completely different or be thrown onto some unholy planet for entering a place where we shouldn't be. I don't know about the rest of you, but this place is beginning to freak me out."

"Calm down, Helen," Sheila said, taking her hand and trying to console her. "I'm sure nothing like that will happen. After all, we've come this far, and we're all still here and in one piece."

"Okay, I'm sure I'm being silly," Helen said, trying to convince herself that she was being unnecessarily frightened by nothing.

"All right, gang, remember our saying, 'All for one and one for all.' Well, let's do it," Cory said, and he held out his hand as he had done at the table in the dining hall."

They all placed their hands on his and repeated their saying: "All for one and one for all." And then they looped our elbows together and continued through this dark damp forest.

After many twist and turns, and climbing over fallen trees and jumping over rocks and stumps, they finally saw a light at the end of their long journey through the forest. The closer they got to the opening, the lighter the air felt, which invigorated them and gave them the will to push on harder and faster. They began to hear birds chirping, and the smell of wildflowers lifted their spirits. Soon they heard the sound of water rushing over little rocks in a creek nearby, and now they began to see even more sunlight as the trees opened up to reveal their way out of this foreboding jungle. They quickly ran out into the sunlight and to the little stream for a nice refreshing drink of water, which filled them with a renewed desire to go on to that white building just across the stream and finally find out what it was used for.

Just downstream a few yards was another small bridge leading straight to that mysterious white building they'd all come so far to investigate.

One by one they each crossed the bridge and walked up a picturesque little path, adorned on each side with pretty purple pansies.

The building was tall and long, with no distinguishing designs or markings on the outside walls. As they walked the length of the building, Sheila called out. "Hay guys, come here. I found a window. There was a small round window like what you would find on a ship. "A port window. I think that's what they call it," Sheila said to the others as they came to see what she had found.

As Sheila peered through the small window, she saw a beautiful room filled with plush pillows and cushions of many lavish colors placed in small groupings all around the room. There were beautiful chandeliers of exquisite crystal hanging over each grouping, and low tables filled with beautiful flowers and bowls of delectable fruits were placed before each grouping of pillows.

Sheila squealed with delight as she said, "It looks just like a royal palace. You must see this." She moved out of the way so Helen could peer in.

"No it doesn't," Helen said as she looked through the window. To her it looked like a classroom, with many desks and chairs and a very large black board on the far wall.

"Let me see," Elaine said as she moved in to look through the tiny window.

"What do you see?" Sheila asked, expecting Elaine to confirm what she had seen.

"Why, I see a large kitchen with stainless steel counter tops and stainless steel appliances. There are many pots and pans and cooking utensils hung neatly above the stoves."

Dumfounded by what each person was seeing, Cory and Elliott both tried peering through the window at the same time.

"You first, Elliott," Cory said. "What do you see?"

"I see a fancy garage with everything you would need to build whatever kind of vehicle you would want. What do you see Cory?"

Cory took his turn. "I see a stage with red velvet curtains and lots of tables and chairs placed in front of it. It looks like a dinner playhouse to me."

"How can this be?" Elliott said. "How can we all look through the same window and see something different?"

"I don't know, Cory said. "But we've got to get in there and see for ourselves exactly what's in there. Look for a door."

They each searched the outside walls of this large white building for a way to get in by running their hands along the wall, hoping to find some hidden entrance. All of a sudden, Helen yelled out, "I've found it. Come quick!" As Helen ran her hands across the surface of the outside wall, the outline of a door appeared, and above the door was a sign that read, Hall of Desires: Do Not Enter Unescorted.

"Wow, you've found it," Elaine said excitedly. "Let go in."

"I don't know," Sheila said. "Did you read the sign above the door?"

"Yeah, but we aren't unescorted," said Cory. "We have each other to escort us through the building."

"I don't know," said Sheila. "I think it means we should have an enlightened one to escort us."

"Well if you want to stay out here while we go in, you can," Helen said. "But I want to see for myself what this building is all about. So who's going in with me?" She looked to the rest of their little group.

"I'm going in," Cory said.

"Me too," said Elliott. "How about you, Elaine. Are you with us?"

"You bet. I wouldn't miss this for anything," she said.

"I'll just wait out here while you guys do your exploring," Sheila said as she sat down on a nice clump of grass next a flowerbed that bordered a path along the length of the white building.

Sheila had an uneasy feeling that it was not a good idea to go snooping around this building without permission, and it was bad enough that she was even a part of this expedition to find out what was in this strange building, let alone entering without the proper escort like the sign said.

"Okay, suit yourself," Cory said. "Let's go."

He pushed the door inward because it didn't have a doorknob on the outside, and it heavily and slowly swung open.

After the last person entered the building, the door swung closed again, and the outline of the door disappeared.

Once in, and with the door closed behind them, Elliott, Cory, Helen, and Elaine found themselves in a narrow but totally white hallway made of smooth pure white marble. The hallway was only wide enough for two people to walk side by side. So Cory and Helen proceeded first with Elliott and Elaine following close behind.

As they proceeded down the hallway, they ran their hands across the smooth hard marble, because the whiteness of the walls made it impossible to tell where one wall ended and another began.

It wasn't long before Helen called out, "The wall on my side has turned to the right." So Cory turned with her down another narrow corridor with Elaine and Elliott close behind.

After walking several yards, they abruptly came to a dead end, realizing this only by walking smack dab into a hard marble wall, nearly knocking them down.

After composing themselves, they turned around and started back down the narrow hallway that they had just come up, only to find that this time the wall turned in the opposite direction. So they took that corridor, thinking it must surly take them to that room they saw from the window when they were outside. And again, it wasn't long before they found themselves at another dead end.

"This is turning out to be a big white labyrinth," Elaine cried out in despair. "I don't think we will ever get out of here."

"No, don't worry about it, Elaine," Cory said. "We have to be getting close. There can't be that many corridors in this place."

"But even if we do find that room, what then?" Helen said. "How will we find our way out of this godforsaken place?" she cried.

"She's right," Elliott said with a heavy sigh. "I think it's time we tried to find our way out, because we have a long walk back to the dorms."

He tried to sound brave, but he too was beginning to get worried that they might not find their way back to the door.

Now as the four slowly and carefully walked the narrow white corridors, they each ran their hands across the walls, trying to find the next passageway in hopes that it would be the way out, but with each corridor they went down, they came to same dreaded dead end. It was beginning to look hopeless, and Elaine and Helen both began to cry.

As Sheila waited for the other four to emerge from the building, she began to get worried. She looked at the sun, now beginning its descent, as dusk was fast approaching. She called out to her friends, saying each of their names, and then she waited for a response. She got none. She tried calling a second and a third time and still got no response. This really worried her, and she knew something must be wrong.

The door was no longer visible, so she decided she'd better mark the area where they had last seen the door so it could be found again. Sheila found a rather large rock and placed it in the approximate location of the door and made an arrow pointing to that location with several smaller rocks, she then decided she had better go now to get help, so she herself wouldn't get lost trying to find her way back to the dorms.

Finally after reaching the courtyard in front of her dorm, she saw Lancer sitting on the bench waiting for her and the others to return.

***

"Lancer, thank God I found you," Sheila said, out of breath from running most of the way.

"What's wrong, Sheila?" I said as I reached for her hands to help her sit on the bench where I'd been sitting.

"The others, Helen, Elaine, Cory, and Elliott, went into the white building a long time ago, and they never came out. I fear something is terribly wrong. I called out to them and got no answer. The door disappeared, but I marked where it's supposed to be." She hardly took a breath between words.

"Calm down, Sheila my dear," I said as I patted her hand with one of mine and wiped her wayward curls from her face with the other. "We will go tell Doshi Tow what you've told me, and he will know what to do."

Just then, without so much as a word of warning, a blaze of white light exploded in a puff of gray smoke before Sheila and me. Once the smoke cleared, there stood Doshi Tow in his orange robes with a stern look on his face.

"What's this I hear about your friends being lost in a white building?" he said, addressing his question at Sheila.

Sheila nervously repeated what she had told me and then apologized for going there in the first place.

Doshi's face softened, and he patted Sheila on the head and said, "Don't you worry, my child. I will see to your friends, and they will be back in their dorms before you know it, safe and sound and no worse for wear, I can assure you. I'm glad you had the good sense not to go into the white building unescorted." He gave her a wink as he again vanished in a flame of bright light."

Chapter 22

Everything Is One

Early the next morning, while it was still quite dark outside, I quietly stole my way to the front lawn of the dorm to sit quietly on the cool soft grass and meditate before everyone else awoke. I made sure, as I left my dorm room, not to disturb Cory, as I softly closed the door behind me. I silently thanked Doshi for rescuing my friends from the white building the night before as I descended the stairs leading to the massive doors that led outside.

I found a nice spot under the canopy of a large maple tree facing the dorm doors to sit in quiet meditation before everyone else began to stir.

As I sat with my legs folded in the lotus position, making sure my spine was erect, with my head sitting square on my shoulders, I closed my eyes and focused my attention at the spot of the spiritual eye, directly in the center of my forehead but just slightly above my eyebrows. I quietly chanted the sacred syllable of *Om* three times, and then I drifted off into a deep and blissful meditation.

The silence of my mind and the stillness of all thoughts began to give way to an amazing awareness in my entire being. I became aware of every cell of my own body working ceaselessly in their very own pre-programmed function to make and then sustain my completely healthy working body. It was like each tiny cell knew exactly what its mission was and executed it with precision, exactness, and flawlessness.

As my mind expanded, I seemed to be witnessing my body as if it were a complete universe unto itself. There were millions, if not billions, of tiny light explosions killing off some cells, while other great flashes of electrical current created new cells in their place. It was like a great battle of good versus evil and the good cells were winning the war. I realized

132

I could not see my whole body as one form, with individual parts, such as organs, skin, eyes, hair, etc. But I knew instinctively that all these hard working cells were my body, and yet each cell had an intelligence all its own.

Just then, another greater awareness came to me. I became aware that even though each tiny cell had its own intelligence and was aware of the function it must complete in order to create its part of the whole body, I also knew that all of these cells and their individual intelligences were, in fact, one with a greater consciousness, and that divine consciousness dwelt in me, but not only me—it also dwelt in all beings everywhere. I then realized that this greater divine consciousness wasn't just in creatures that were alive. It was also living in inanimate objects. These living cells, with their explosive power, which were moving under their own intelligence, also created all inanimate objects, such as stones, buildings, metals, and also things that had died, such as bodies and trees and plants, giving me the awareness that everything was living and dying and then being reborn into something else again and again, over and over, with no end.

Just then, I heard Cory and Elliott calling my name. "Lancer, wake up man," Elliott said as he nudged me on my shoulder.

"Yeah, Lance, are you in there?" Cory said, half-jokingly. "You need to get up so we can go to class."

"Huh? Okay, man we have plenty of time," I said to Cory and Elliott as I stretched out my legs so I could stand up.

"No we don't. We've been trying to wake you up for the last hour, but you were like some kind of zombie or something," Elliott said.

"What? How can that be? It felt like I only just sat down," I said as I looked at my watch? "We had better get going, or we'll be late." I jumped to my feet and brushed off my pants, amazed that the time had flown by so fast during my meditation.

Cory handed me my journal, and we all took off running to Doshi's class, which he had promised would be a class we didn't want to miss.

Chapter 23

Training The Mind

Arriving barely on time, Cory, Elliott, and I were the last ones to enter the class and be seated. Sheila gave me a stern look as she leaned over from her seat to ask me what took us so long.

"I will have to tell you later," I said as Doshi now rang the bell, letting us all know it was time to start our class.

"I'm glad you could all make it on time," Doshi said as he mischievously threw a glance toward Elliott, Cory, and me. But then he started right in, not wanting to waste a minute of this very important class we were going to have today.

"Today we are going to be training the mind so that you will be able to use it in the most effective ways to accomplish whatever goal you have set out to do. For instance, say you need to get into a building to help someone in need and all the doors and windows are locked. Today you will begin to learn how to use your mind to transform your physical body so that you can go through a wall to get to the one who needs your help. We will also be learning how to levitate, turn invisible, bilocate, or anything you could possibly dream up that you would like to be able to do. You will find out that, through the instrument of the mind, all possibilities are not only possible but are actually already a reality for those who have learned to expand their minds in complete faith, letting go of everything that they thought they knew. In this class, you will have to unlearn everything you were taught by your parents, friends, teachers, and acquaintances before you came here. You will become aware of truth, and with truth, nothing is impossible.

"The first thing I would like you all to do is stand and form two lines. All girls to the right and all boys to the left please. We will have a contest to see which of you are the most enlightened among the boys and girls." Doshi had an amused look on his face.

Since Sheila and I were on the front row, we each were the first ones in line in our two groups.

Doshi then stood at the front of the class between our two groups, and he raised both of his arms out to the sides. Then, miraculously, out of the blue, without any bright lightning flashes or smoke like we were used to seeing when one of the enlightened teachers did something out of the ordinary, two brick walls appeared. One stood before the girls' line and one before the boys' line.

"Now this is an exercise to see who can materialize themselves on the other side of this wall without going around it," Doshi explained. "You must first concentrate your attention at the spiritual eye and visualize yourself being on the other side, and if you have great concentration, keeping all other thoughts from interfering, then you should be able to accomplish this small task."

For some reason, I had no doubt that I could do this, so I brought my focus between my eyebrows and saw myself standing on the other side of this brick wall smiling at Doshi Tow. The next thing I knew, Doshi Tow was clapping and congratulating me on successfully completing this task. Then, a few minutes later, Sheila appeared on the other side of her wall. Doshi also congratulated her, and we sat back down, waiting for the rest of the kids to complete the same task. Some did all right but took longer than Sheila and I, and there were some that, no matter how hard they tried, just weren't able to do it. So while Doshi was working with them, he bilocated to those of us that had already done it and told us we could work on doing other things while he helped the students who couldn't manage to get through the wall yet.

Sheila asked, "Lancer, why don't we take turns trying out new things with our minds?"

"Like what?"

The next thing I knew Sheila's body was lifting off the floor. She was actually levitating, and she said, "Like this, silly. Now you try it."

So again, I visualized myself floating about six inches higher than Sheila, and sure enough, there I was. It was like child's play to me, and I was amazed at how simple all this was coming to me.

Sheila laughed as we came back to our seats.

As we looked around the room, we saw some other students levitating, while others seemed to stretch out their arms clear across the room to get something without getting up.

"Wow, this is pretty fun," I said as I presented Sheila with a beautiful bouquet of flowers that I had so vividly imagined.

And she accepted them happily with an instant flush of pink in her cheeks. "Why, thank you, Mr. Puckett." She curtsied in gratitude for my gift.

Everyone in the class was having so much fun trying new things that laughter could be heard from every part of the room. Some kids, however, were having a hard time and were failing to accomplish their intended goals, but they never gave up trying. But for the most part, it was such a fun class that the time just flew by, and everyone was surprised when Doshi Tow rang his bell.

"Attention, my dear children," he said. "Some of you still need to sharpen the focus of your minds, so I will work with you so you can deepen your meditation in our future classes. By deepening your meditations, you will learn to visualize more clearly, for it is through visualization that all things were brought forth, and it is through this means that all things are possible."

Doshi went on to say, "The divine consciousness is pure imagination, which first had to be visualized before anything was ever brought into existence. So it is vitally important that you all learn this art. However, I've been watching all of you, and I'm pleased to say there are some in this class who are ready to start their first assignments on the earth plain." Doshi had a twinkle in his eye as he glanced at Sheila and me.

"I've not only been watching you during our class time together, but I've been aware of all of your activities whether you were physically with me or not, and those of you who will be starting your first assignments will find your names on a list in the dining hall after the evening meal. It will explain where you need to go and when you will be expected. Thank you very much, my dear children. Class is dismissed for today."

Chapter 24

The Chosen Ones

"I wonder who Doshi was talking about when he said there are some in our class who were ready for their first assignment on earth," Cory asked as he and Elliott walked with Helen and Elaine just in front of Sheila and me on our way to our afternoon meal.

"I saw him glance at Lancer and Sheila," Elaine exclaimed as she threw a backward glance at us.

"I don't know about Sheila," Cory said. "But Lancer—I think not! He's always getting himself into something he should stay out of. Don't you remember, guys? He was just called to the counselor's office not long ago. So I'm quite sure it couldn't be Lancer, Doshi was talking about." He had a bit of sarcasm in his voice, trying to be funny as he looked back in our direction.

"Ha, ha, Cory," I said. "That's real funny. But I'm sure you're right. I don't feel at all qualified yet to have my first assignment. Sheila, on the other hand, is very smart, and it wouldn't surprise me at all if she was one of the people Doshi was talking about."

Helen inserted herself into the conversation, saying, "I saw some pretty fantastic things being done by quite a few of the other students in our class, so it wouldn't surprise me if Doshi was talking about some of them and not any of us at all."

"We'll all find out who it is soon enough," Sheila chimed in, as if to say we'd had enough talk on this subject. Then she grabbed hold of Helen's arm, pulling her with her as she hastened her pace. Looking back briefly at the rest of us, she said, "I don't know about the rest of you, but I'm starving. Let's go."

As we entered the great dining hall, Elliott playfully shoved Cory, who almost fell over. He would have if it were not for Helen catching him before he tumbled forward. "I sure hope it's a good meal today," said Elliott. "Because it might be the last meal we get to eat together for some of us."

"Okay, settle down, Elliott. Eventually all of us will have our first assignment, so don't make such a big deal out of it, man," Cory said.

As we sat at our table with steaming hot trays full of an assortment of savory foods, everyone started eating, as if they just couldn't get enough. All except me, that is. I was thinking about that strange but wonderful experience I'd had earlier that morning in my meditation on the front lawn before class.

As I thought about what had happened to me, I began again to feel a strange but enjoyable tingling in my brain, starting from the base of my skull and going to the top of my head. Now, as I looked at my companions, who were happily carrying on a conversation and enjoying their food, I began to see them from a completely different perspective. I saw each of their forms, but they were no longer physical beings made of flesh and bones. Instead I saw them as billions of tiny active cells doing their thing, and each of these cells had a consciousness of its own. They all had a job to do, and they were doing it. I also saw that I was a conglomerate of tiny individual cells, working together to create the completed structure that made me who I was. As I looked at the food my friends were eating, I realized that those cells weren't any different from those that made up the bodies of my friends. They only vibrated at a different speed from those that formed the human body. Thus it was the vibrational speed of the cells that created different physical forms. It was amazing to actually see and experience how all the cells and molecules worked together with an intelligence all their own. Each cell would fire off electrical charges, which created a multitude of tiny light particles that seemed to dart back and forth until they collided with another light particle that matched their own, and then they would merge together to build a bigger particle until it grew into a molecule, and on and on it went.

Suddenly I heard Cory say, "Snap out of it, Lancer buddy. There you go again, signing off as if you're in some kind of trance or something. What's wrong with you man?" Cory snapped his fingers in front of my face.

Immediately the physical world came back into focus when I heard Cory calling me and snapping his fingers. "Oh, I'm sorry, guys. I was just thinking about something, but it's no big deal. This food sure looks good today." I tried to quickly change the subject."

"Is there something you want to tell us, Lance my boy?" Cory asked as he leaned across the table to get a good look in my eyes, as if staring at me square in the face would make me talk.

"No, I was just thinking about the meditation I had this morning, that all. And it's something I just think I should keep to myself for now. So lets drop it and enjoy the meal."

The rest of our mealtime went wonderful, with all of us happily talking about all the adventures we'd had since we crossed over into this new sphere of existence after our untimely deaths.

"Now that we're done with lunch, we'd better check out the new list, to see if any of us are on it. I'm not sure I would want to be one of the first ones to have an assignment on earth," Elliott said as he scooted himself away from the table. The sentiment was affirmed, by the rest of our little group as we headed down the hall to where all bulletins, memos, and lists were always posted.

This time, there were only two lists for new assignments. One was for girls, and the other was for the boys. As we scrolled down the lists, looking for our names, which again were in alphabetical order, I saw it. There it was. I was hoping it wouldn't be there, but, alas, my name seemed to protrude right off the paper at me: Lancer Puckett, in bold black letters. The instructions next to my name told me again to go to the counselor's office immediately. It was the same room I'd been to before—room 101. I remembered that Shakti had been my counselor before and wondered if she would be there again.

Elliott and Cory searched several times for their names, thinking they may have overlooked them, but fortunately for them, their names were not anywhere on the list. Elliott breathed a heavy sigh of relief, and Cory lightly frowned in disappointment at not being chosen.

"Well, buddy," Cory said as he slapped the back of my shoulder. "It looks like I was wrong about you after all. Who would have ever thought that you would be first to go?"

"I guess so," I said, not knowing what else to say.

"That's okay," Elliott said, acting a bit macho. "I guess we'll just have to catch up with you later, bro. He swung his arm around my neck, putting me in a playful headlock."

Just then, Sheila, Elaine, and Helen met up with us and told us what they had found out. Helen and Elaine almost simultaneously spilled out the fact that Sheila had been chosen, but they had not. Sheila lowered her eyes, not out of shame but out of humility. And she didn't want to make such a big thing of it.

"Well, well. It looks like the two love birds made it," Cory said with a playful smirk.

At that, Sheila raised her eyes and looked at me with a slight smile on her full lips, thankful that I had been chosen too.

"Well, guys," I said. "My instructions said that I was to go immediately to the counselor's room again so I'd better get going."

"Mine said the same thing Sheila quickly said, not wanting to be left behind if I was going too."

"What is your room number?" I asked.

"It's room 101," she said.

"That's great. We can walk together," I said, and we both said our good-byes to the others and headed to room 101.

Once there, again I noticed there was no doorknob on the door, but there was a sign that said please come in and be seated. Sheila tried to push open the door but it wouldn't open, so I suggested that we try what we had learned about visualizing ourselves on the other side, and she agreed.

So we held hands and focused our minds on the spiritual eye and visualized ourselves on the other side of the door, and the next thing we knew, we were standing inside room 101.

"Good afternoon, Lancer. Good afternoon, Sheila," Shakti said as she stood next to Lord Aster, Doshi Tow, and Estrella.

"We are so please with your progress that it is our opinion that you two are the first two enrollees in our spirit guide class who are already ready for an assignment on the earth plane."

"There are a few things that you yet have to learn," Doshi said. "For instance, your environment is not a separate thing from you. It is the result of your perceptive patterns, and these are determined by psychological structures in each of your minds. It will be your job to create the proper structure so as to improve the environment and thus improve the situation of those individuals you are sent to help. You must remember that there are no limitations to the self and there are no limitations to its potentials. Because, as you know, the self is not your physical body, the real self is spirit, and with spirit all things are possible, he said. Most people develop or adopt artificial limitations through their own ignorance, and they identify with them so deeply that this causes them great pain and misery in their lives. And you two will be sent to help them change their artificial limitations so that they can heal and grow, both mentally and spiritually."

"We all have great faith in your abilities," Lord Aster said with a sparkle in his eyes as he raised, then lowered his bushy eyebrows and caressed his beard. Then he gave us an approving smile. "You have been given perhaps the most awesome gift of all from the creator of all that is, and that is this: the ability to project your thoughts outward into physical form. This gift has also been given to each human being throughout the galaxies and in every solar system. All people everywhere have the same ability as you, but they are unaware of this great gift, and until they are able to change their thought structures or patterns with your help, they will be ever in a state of suffering. It is your job not to take away their suffering but to help them change their thought patterns so that they can end their own suffering."

Estrella then stepped forward and placed the third finger from her right hand in a little jar of Vibhuti that she held in her left hand, and then she placed that finger on the spot of the spiritual eye on Sheila's forehead for a few seconds. Then she did the same to me. At that very moment, I could feel a great energy surge through my body and then come to rest in my mind. My entire brain seemed to be electrified with energy that seemed to draw in information from far reaching sources never before known to me. I felt more alive and stronger than I had ever felt before. As I looked at Sheila I could tell that she felt the same way I did.

Shakti again asked if we were ready for our first assignment, and we nodded in the affirmative, too overwhelmed with this new sense of power and knowledge to say anything with real words.

Then Shakti, Lord Aster, Doshi Tow, and Estrella made a circle around Sheila and me and asked us to face each other. They then held each other's hands and began chanting the sacred syllable *Om* over and over again. Then the room became illuminated with a brilliant white light, and we could feel the vibration of the powerful syllable *Om* living and breathing in us as we stood facing each other. In the very next moment, our minds merged together, and then we were gone! Sheila and I were headed for our first assignment, not knowing where or what kind of assignment it would be.